HEROIC ADVENTURE AT ITS BEST

Stark grasped his own ankle, found the odd hand that did not belong there, and shifted his grip to the alien wrist. And all the time he and the sea-thing were plunging deeper, the milky light growing dimmer.

The arm was long and furred, and powerful muscles were imbedded in a layer of fat. Stark's grip kept slipping, and he knew that if he lost it he was finished. His fingers clawed and tore, moving convulsively toward the point of leverage.

The smooth descent stopped. The creature turned its head and Stark saw the blurred face, eyes filmed and staring, bubbles trickling from a vestigial nose. The free arm that had been oaring them downward now swung over, not toward his hands but toward the back of his neck. The game was over . . .

"Imaginatively, Brackett is absolutely at the top of her genre, filling this book as full of marvels, personalities, strange customs, and hair-raising escapes as a Christmas pudding is full of plums. Of its kind, it's just delicious."

—Publishers Weekly

BOOKS BY LEIGH BRACKETT
Published by Ballantine Books

THE BEST OF LEIGH BRACKETT

THE BOOK OF SKAITH
  Volume One: THE GINGER STAR
  Volume Two: THE HOUNDS OF SKAITH
  Volume Three: THE REAVERS OF SKAITH

THE LONG TOMORROW

THE STARMEN OF LLYRDIS

THE
GINGER STAR

Volume One of
The Book of Skaith

LEIGH BRACKETT

A Del Rey Book

BALLANTINE BOOKS • NEW YORK

A somewhat shorter version of this novel was serialized in the magazine *Worlds of IF*, Copyright © 1974 by UPD Publishing Corporation.

A Del Rey Book
Published by Ballantine Books

ISBN 0-345-28514-X

Manufactured in the United States of America

First Edition: May 1974
Third Printing: December 1979

First Canadian Printing: May 1974

Map by Bob Porter

Cover art by Boris Vallejo

For Robert and Cecelia

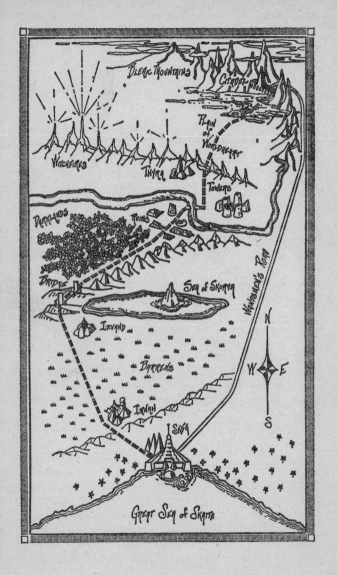

1

Stark got his final view of Pax from the tender, going out to the spaceport moon, and that was the best view he had had of it. Pax is the chief habitable planet of Vega. It is also a city, and the proud boast of that hopefully and precariously christened world is that not one single grain of corn grows upon it, nor is one single useful item manufactured.

The city soars up into the sky. It spreads out over every landmass and swallows up small seas. It burrows underground, level upon level. Large areas of it are especially conditioned and equipped for non-humans. Everything comes into it from the outside. All supplies are shipped to the lunar docks and brought on down by freight tenders. Nothing lives on Pax but bureaucrats, diplomats, and computers.

Pax is the administrative center of the Galactic Union, a democratic federation of star-worlds flung across half the Milky Way and including, very incidentally, the worlds of little Sol. In this place the millions of problems besetting billions of people inhabiting thousands of diverse planets are reduced to tidy and easily manageable abstractions on tapes, cards, and endless sheets of paper.

A paper world, Stark thought, full of paper people.

Simon Ashton was not made of paper. Time, and accomplishments in planetary administration, had promoted him to a comfortable office at the Ministry of Planetary Affairs and a comfortable apartment in a mile-high building which he need not ever leave, if he did not wish to, except to take one of the moving walkways to work. Still, like many of his colleagues in that Ministry, Ashton had never lost his rawhide, taut-wire energy. He often went into the field, knowing that the problems of actual beings in actual places could not be solved merely by the regurgitation of data from a bank of clacking machines.

He had gone once too often into the field. He had not come back.

Stark received that information on one of the unlicked worlds outside the Union, where life was a little more relaxed for people like himself. He was, as the old phrase had it, a wolf's-head—a totally masterless man in a society where everyone respectable *belonged* to something. He bestowed his allegiance only where he chose, usually for pay. He was a mercenary by trade, and there were enough little wars going on both in and out of the Union, enough remote peoples calling on him for the use of his talents, so that he was able to make a reasonable living doing what he did best.

Fighting.

He had begun fighting almost before he could stand. Born in a mining colony in Mercury's Twilight Belt, he had fought to live on a planet that did not encourage life; his parents were dead, his foster-parents a tribe of sub-human aboriginals clawing a precarious existence out of the sun-stricken valleys. He had fought, without success, the men who slaughtered those foster-parents and put him in a cage, a snarling curiosity. Later on, he had fought for a different kind of survival, the survival of himself as a man.

He would never have got past square one without Simon Ashton.

He could remember vividly the heat, the raw pain of loss, the confinement of the bars, the men who laughed and tormented him. Then Ashton came, Ashton the wielder of authority, the savior, and that was the beginning of the life of Eric John Stark, as distinguished from N'Chaka, the Man-Without-a-Tribe.

Now twice-orphaned, Eric/N'Chaka gradually accepted Ashton as his father-in-being. More than that, he accepted Ashton as his friend. The years of his grow-ing-up were associated almost solely with Ashton be-cause they had been much alone in the frontier stations to which Ashton was sent. Ashton's kindness, his coun-sel, his patience, his strength and his affection were stamped indelibly on the fibers of Stark's being. He had gotten even his name through Ashton, who had searched the records of Mercury Metals and Mining to track down his parents.

And now Simon Ashton was missing, disappeared, on the world of a ginger star somewhere at the back of be-yond, out in the Orion Spur. A newly discovered, newly opened world called Skaith that hardly anyone had ever heard of, except at Galactic Center. Skaith was not a member of the Union but there had been a consulate. Someone had called to the Union for help, and Ashton was the man who went to see about it.

Ashton had, perhaps, exceeded his authority. Even so, his superiors had done their best. But the local powers closed the consulate and refused entrance to of-ficers of the Union. All attempts to discover Ashton's whereabouts, or the reason for his disappearance, had ended at a blank wall.

Stark caught the first available ship outbound for Gal-actic center and Pax. Looking for Ashton had become his personal business.

The weeks he had spent at Pax had been neither pleasant nor easy. He had had to do a great deal of talk-ing and convincing and, after that, much learning. He was glad to be leaving, impatient to get on with the job.

The world-city dropped behind him, and he breathed more freely. Presently the enormous intricacies of the lunar spaceport engulfed him, sorted him, tagged him and eventually spewed him into the bowels of a trim little cargo liner which took him about a third of the way to his destination. Three more changes were scheduled af-ter that, progressively downward, into a rickety old tramp—the only sort of ship that served Skaith.

He endured the voyage, continuing by means of tapes the education into things Skaithian he had begun at Pax. He was not popular among his fellow travelers. His cabin mate complained that he twitched and growled in his sleep like an animal, and there was something in the gaze of his pale eyes that disconcerted them. They called him "the wild man" behind his back and ceased trying to lure him into games, the discussions of schemes for turning a quick profit, or personal reminiscences.

The tramp trader made several planet falls along the way. But eventually it creaked and rattled out of FTL drive within sight of a solar system lost in the wilderness of Orion Spur.

It was the fourth month, by Galactic Arbitrary Time, after Ashton's disappearance.

Stark destroyed his tapes and collected his few belongings. The rickety trader settled down on the rickety starport at Skeg, the only one on the planet, and discharged its passengers.

Stark was the first man off the ship.

His papers gave his right name, which meant nothing here, but they did not mention Pax as a point of origin for his flight. They said that he was an Earthman, which he was in a way, and a dealer in rarities, which he was not. At the barrier shed a couple of surly men confiscated his purely defensive stunner—he could have it back, they said, when he left—and searched him and his meager luggage for other weapons. He was then given a terse lecture, in bad Universal, on the rules and regulations governing life in Skeg and was sent on his way with the parting information that all roads out of Skeg except the one leading to the starport were closed to off-worlders. He was not under any circumstances to leave the city.

He rode the ten miles in a jolting cart, past plantations of tropical fruits, waterlogged paddies where some form of grain was growing lushly, and patches of jungle. Gradually the smell of mud and vegetation was overlaid by a smell of sea water, salty and stagnant. Stark did not like it much.

When the cart topped a low line of jungled hills, he found that he did not much like the look of the sea, either. Skaith had no moon, so there were no tides to stir it, and there was a milky, greasy sheen to the surface. Skaith's old ginger-colored sun was going down in a senile fury of crimson and molten brass, laying streaks of unhealthy brilliance across the water. The sea seemed a perfect habitat for the creatures who were said to live in it.

Beside the sea, on the bank of a river, was Skeg. The river had grown thin with age, too weak to do more than trickle through a narrow passage where the silt of centuries had all but closed its mouth. A ruined fortress-tower was set on low cliffs to guard a vanished harbor. But the city itself looked lively enough, with lamps and torches glowing out as the sun sank.

Presently, Stark saw the first of the Three Ladies, magnificent star-clusters—the ornament of Skaith's night skies—that made it impossible to come by a decent darkness. He glowered at the Lady, admiring her beauty but thinking that she and her sisters could make things very difficult for him.

As though the situation would not be difficult enough.

The cart eventually came clumping into the town. Skeg was one great open market where almost anything could be bought or sold, and the streets were busy. Shops and stalls were brightly lighted. Vendors with barrows cried their wares. People from all over the Fertile Belt—tall, leather-clad warrior-burghers from the outlying city-states as well as the small silken folk of the tropics—mingled with the off-worlders who came to traffic, exchanging precious foreign items like iron pigs for drugs, or artifacts looted from Skaith's plentiful supply of ruins.

And of course there were the Farers. Everywhere. A conglomerate of all the races, dressed or undressed in every imaginable fashion, trooping about, lying about, doing whatever happened to occur to them at the moment; the careless itinerant children of the Lords Protector, who neither toiled nor spun, but blew lightly with the winds of the world. Stark noticed some off-worlders among them, drifters who had found the good life here in the warm twilight of a planet where everything went and where, if you belonged to the right groups, everything was free.

Stark paid off his driver and found lodgings at an inn catering to off-worlders. The room was small but reasonably clean, and the food, when he sampled it, not at all bad.

In any case, he was not interested in comfort. He was interested in Ashton.

When he had eaten, he approached the landlord in the common-room of the inn, which was built in the breezy tropical style of Skeg, being mostly windows with reed curtains that rolled down to shut out the rain. It was not raining now, and the sea wind blew through, heavy and damp.

"How do I find the Galactic Union consulate?"

The landlord stared at him. He was a dark purple in color, with a face of stone and startlingly light, very cold gray eyes.

"The consulate? Didn't you know?"

"Know what?" asked Stark, looking suitably blank.

"There isn't one. Not any more."

"But I was told—"

"The Farers wrecked it, not quite four months ago. Sent the consul and his staff packing. They—"

"The Farers?"

"Surely you were told about them at the starport. All that human garbage littering up the streets."

"Oh, yes," said Stark. "I was just surprised. They seem—well, too indolent."

"All they need is the word," said the landlord sourly. "When the Wandsmen say go, they go."

Stark nodded. "I was warned about the Wandsmen,

too. Pain of death and all that. They seem to be very important men on Skaith."

"They do the dirty work for the Lords Protector. The Chief Wandsman of Skeg, the almighty Gelmar, led the Farers. He told the consul to get gone and stay gone, they wanted no more outside interference. In fact, for a while it seemed they might kick us all out and close the starport. They didn't, quite. Needed the imports too badly. But they treat us like criminals."

"I got the feeling that foreigners weren't popular," Stark said. "What was the row about?"

The landlord shook his head. "Some damned official busybody from Pax. It's a fairly open secret that he was here to arrange emigration from one of the city-states. More fool he."

"Oh? What happened to him?"

"Who knows? Except the Wandsmen." The cold eyes regarded Stark suspiciously. "Got a particular interest?"

"Hardly."

"Then drop the subject. We've had trouble enough already. What did you want with the consulate, anyway?"

"Some routine business about travel papers. It'll have to wait till my next port of call."

He bade the landlord good night and walked out.

Some damned busybody from Pax.

Ashton.

And only the Wandsmen knew what had happened to him.

Stark had made that assumption himself, some time ago, so he was not downcast. He had not expected to walk into Skeg and find signs posted to tell him his way.

He walked through the crowded streets, a dark man in a dark tunic—a big man, powerfully muscled, who carried himself as lightly and easily as a dancer. He was in no hurry. He let the city flow around him, absorbing it through all the senses, including one that civilized men have largely lost. But he was not civilized. He was aware of the lights, the colors, the mingled smells, the strange musics made by unnameable instruments and alien voices, the bright banners that hung above the sin-shops, the movements of people; underneath it all he sensed a rich, ripe stink of decay. Skaith was dying, of course, but it did not seem to him to be dying well.

He could see no reason to delay sticking his head into the noose, and so presently he entered a tavern and began his work.

He went about it most discreetly. He had spent what felt like an eternity at Pax, going with cold bitter patience through all the existing information on Skaith— learning the language, learning as much as was known about the people and their customs, talking to the ex-consul in an effort to learn more. It was already, of course, too late to save Ashton—had been too late from the moment he disappeared—if the Wandsmen had decided he should die. Two possibilities remained: rescue or revenge. For either one, Stark needed all the knowledge he could get.

It was not extensive. Contact with Skaith had only occurred a dozen or so years ago, and the consulate was not established until five years later. Much was known about Skeg and the adjacent country. Something was known about the city-states. Very little was known about the lands beyond the Fertile Belt, where most of the population of Skaith was now gathered. He had heard tall tales about the Barrens and the People of the Barrens, and perhaps some of them were true, and perhaps not.

Nothing was known about the Lords Protector, in the sense that no one knew exactly what they looked like or exactly where they dwelt—no one except the Wandsmen, who kept this knowledge as a high and holy secret. The beliefs of various sects and cults only confused matters. The consul's report had said:

"The Lords Protector, reputed to be 'undying and unchanging,' were apparently established long ago by the then ruling powers, as a sort of super-benevolence. The Great Migrations were beginning, the civilizations of the north were breaking up as the people moved away from the increasing cold, and there was certain to be a time of chaos with various groups competing for new lands. Then and later, when some stability was re-established, the Lords Protector were to prevent too great a trampling of the weak by the strong. Their law was simple: to succor the weak, to feed the hungry, to shelter the homeless, to strive always toward the greatest good of the greatest number.

"It appears that through the centuries this law has been carried far beyond its original intent. The Farers and the many smaller non-productive fragments of this thoroughly fragmented culture are now the greater number, with the result that the Wandsmen, in the name of the Lords Protector, hold a third or more of the population in virtual slavery to supply the rest.

"It is quite obvious to me that when the Wandsmen learned of the intention of the Irnanese to emigrate, they took immediate and violent action to prevent it. If Irnan were to accomplish this removal, other communities would surely follow, leaving the Wandsmen and their charges in a sad state. Ashton's disappearance and the forcible closing of the consulate came as a shock to us, but hardly a surprise."

A great deal was known about the Wandsmen.

What Stark wanted to do was seek out Gelmar and tear him slowly and painfully into small bits until he told what he had done to Ashton. This was not possible because of the Farers, the devoted, perpetual, ever-ready, instant mob. So he set himself out as bait.

For two days he walked quietly in the streets and sat quietly in the taverns and talked quietly to anyone who would listen, asking questions, occasionally letting slip the name *Irnan*.

On the evening of the second day the bait was taken.

2

He was in the principal street of Skeg, in the main market square, watching a troupe of acrobats performing indifferent stunts with a minimum of skill, when someone came and stood close to him, very close, warm and breathing.

He looked down. It was a girl—he had known that, of course, from the touch—a Farer, stark naked except for body-paint laid on in fanciful loops and spirals and her hair, which hung over her shoulders like a cloak. She looked up at Stark and smiled.

"My name is Baya," she said. It meant Graceful, and she was. "Come with me."

"Sorry. I'm not in the market."

She continued to smile. "Love can come later, if you wish. Or not, as you wish. But I can tell you something about the man Ashton, who took the road to Irnan."

He said sharply, "What do you know about that?"

"I am a Farer. We know many things."

"Very well, then. Tell me about Ashton."

"Not here. Too many eyes and ears, and that is a forbidden subject."

"Then why are you willing to talk?"

Her eyes and her warm mouth told him why she was willing. "Besides, I don't care for rules, any rules. You know the old fortress? Go there, now. I'll follow."

Stark hesitated, frowning, suspicious.

She yawned and said, "It's up to you."

She drifted away into the crowd. Stark stood a moment, then began to walk casually along the street, toward the lower end where it narrowed into a quiet lane and came at last to the river.

A bridge had been here once, but now there was only a ford paved with stones. A man dressed in a yellow robe picked his way across it, his skirts tucked up and his wet thighs flashing. Half a dozen men and women followed him in a body, holding each other's hands. Stark turned onto the broken pavement of the embankment.

The fortress was ahead, with the sea lapping the cliffs below it. The ginger star was setting in the same lurid manner as before; gaudy sunsets seemed the normal thing here. The tideless water gleamed, gradually taking on a sheen of pearl. Things swirled and splashed in it, and a strange, far-off sound of hooting voices made Stark shiver. The consul had dutifully written down what had been told to him about the Children of the Sea-Our-Mother, but he obviously had not believed it. Stark kept an open mind.

Even a stupid animal would have known it was heading into a trap, and Stark was not stupid. The ancient walls of the fortress towered beside him, still with the stillness of idle centuries, gaping doors and window-places dark and empty. He could hear nothing, see nothing that was threatening, yet the nerves rippled under the skin of his back. He leaned against the stones and waited, tasting the wet rankness of the air.

The girl came, padding on little bare feet. And there was someone with her, a tall man who wore a rich tunic of somber red and carried a wand of office. A man with a high, proud, calm face, a man of power who had never known fear.

"I am Gelmar," he said, "Chief Wandsman of Skeg."

Stark nodded. There did not seem to be anyone near but these two.

"Your name is Eric John Stark," said Gelmar. "An Earthman, like Ashton."

"Yes."

"What are you to Ashton?"

"Friend. Foster-son. I owe him my life." Stark stepped forward. "I want to know what happened to him."

"And perhaps I'll tell you," said Gelmar easily. "But first you must tell me who sent you."

"No one. When I heard that Ashton was missing, I came."

"You speak our language. You know about Irnan. You must have been at Galactic Center, to learn these things."

"I went there to learn."

"And then you came to Skaith because of your love for Ashton."

"Yes."

"I don't think I believe you, Earthman. I think you were sent to make more mischief here."

In the reddening dusk Stark saw that they were looking at him in a very odd way, and when Gelmar spoke again his tone had changed subtly, as though the seemingly innocent questions had a secret importance.

"Who is your master? Ashton? The Ministry?"

Stark said, "I have no master." His breathing now was shallow, his ears stretched for little sounds.

"A wolf's-head," said Gelmar softly. "Where is your home?"

"I have none."

"A landless man." This was beginning to have a ritual sound. "Who are your people?"

"I have none. I was not born on Earth. My other name is N'Chaka, Man-Without-a-Tribe."

Baya sighed, a little sharp sound. "Let me ask him," she said. Her eyes were very bright, catching the afterglow. "A wolf's-head, a landless man, a man without a tribe." She reached out and touched Stark with a small hand, and the fingers were cold as ice. "Will you join with me and be a Farer? Then you will have one master, love. And one home, Skaith. And one people. Us."

Stark said, "No."

She drew back from him, and her eyes seemed to grow brighter with some light of their own.

She said to Gelmar, "He *is* the Dark Man of the prophecy."

Astonished, Stark said, "What prophecy?"

"That is something they could not tell you at Pax," said Gelmar. "The prophecy was not made until after the consul had gone. But we have been waiting for you."

The girl gave a sudden cry, and then Stark heard the sounds he had been expecting.

They came from both sides, around the fortress, perhaps twenty of them, male and female, leaping grotesques of all shapes and sizes. Careless garments flapped. Hands brandished sticks and stones. Some were chanting, "Kill, kill!"

Stark said, "I thought it was forbidden to kill at Skeg."

Gelmar smiled. "Not when I order it."

Baya drew a long pin like a stiletto from the darkness of her hair.

Stark stood, in the second or two that remained to him, looking this way and that like one desperate to find a way of escape. Gelmar moved away toward the edge of the cliff, giving his Farers free room as the stones began to fly.

Out over the water, the hooting voices called and chuckled.

Stark sprang like a wild beast for Gelmar and bore him into the sea.

They sank down to a slimy bottom, and it was instantly apparent that Gelmar could not swim. Small wonder, Stark thought, and held him down relentlessly until his struggles weakened. Then he brought him to the surface and let him breathe. Gelmar stared at him in such shocked amazement that Stark laughed. Upon the cliff the Farers stood, stunned, in a ragged line.

"The Children of the Sea-Our-Mother," Stark said. "I am told they eat men."

"They do," said Gelmar, strangling. "You must be . . . insane . . ."

"What have I to lose?" said Stark, and pushed him under. When he let him up again the last of Gelmar's arrogance was gone, lost in a paroxysm of retching.

The hooting voices had come closer, and there was a new note in them of alert interest, as when hounds pick up a scent.

"Two questions," said Stark. "Is Ashton alive?" Gelmar choked and gagged, and Stark shook him. "Do you want the Children to share you? Answer me!"

Feebly, Gelmar answered. "Yes. Yes. He's alive."

"Do you lie, Wandsman? Shall I drown you?"

"No! Lords Protector . . . wanted him . . . alive. To question. We took him . . . on the road to Irnan."

"Where is he?"

"North. Citadel . . . Lords Protector . . . at World-heart."

The Farers had begun wailing, a collection of banshees. They were forming a human chain down the cliff, reaching out their hands to succor Gelmar. The first of the Three Ladies silvered sky and sea. There was a great and savage joy in Stark's belly.

"Good. Then I will ask a third question. What prophecy?"

"Gerrith . . . wise woman of Irnan." Gelmar was finding his tongue as the seaward sounds came nearer. "She prophesied . . . an off-worlder would come . . . destroy the Lords Protector . . . because of Ashton." The eyes, no longer so proud and calm, yearned toward the cliff.

"Ah," said Stark. "Did she now? And perhaps she was right."

He thrust Gelmar from him, toward the reaching hands, but did not wait to see whether or not he made it. Across the warm and somehow unclean water there were flashes of white in the cluster-light, like many swimmers tossing spray.

Stark kicked off his sandals, put his head down, and made for the opposite shore.

The rush of his own passage blotted out all other noises, yet he knew they were gaining on him. He managed to lengthen his stroke just a fraction more. Then he began to feel the vibrations, a sort of booming in the water as something displaced it with rhythmic blows. He was aware of a body, immensely strong, impossibly swift, pulling ahead of him.

Instead of turning and fleeing blindly, as he was expected to, Stark swerved to the attack.

3

Almost at once, Stark realized that he had made a mistake. Quite possibly, his last one.

He had the advantage of surprise, but that was short-lived. In the matter of strength and reflexes he was as near animal as a man can reasonably be, but the creature he fought with was in its own element. Stark grappled with it and it shot upward from the water like a tarpon, breaking his grip. He saw it briefly above him in the cluster-light, outstretched arms shaking diamond drops, body girdled with foam. It looked down at him, laughing, and its eyes were like pearls. Then it was gone in a curving arc that drove it beneath the surface. Its form was manlike, except that there seemed to be webs of skin in odd places, and the head was earless.

And it was somewhere beneath him now, out of sight. Stark rolled and dived.

The thing circled him round, flashed over him, and again was gone. It was having fun.

Stark came back to the surface. Farther out, the splashing had ceased. He could see heads bobbing about, and hear those hateful voices hooting and ha-ha-ing. For the moment the pack seemed to be standing off, allowing their leader to play out his game.

Stark could see nothing between himself and the shore. He set off toward it again, swimming like one in a panic.

For a little while nothing happened, and the shore was so tantalizingly close that he almost thought he might make it. Then a powerful hand closed on his ankle and drew him smoothly under.

Now he had to hurry.

Recklessly expending strength because there was nothing to save it for, he bent his knees, doubling his body against the thrust of the water that wanted to keep it stretched. He grasped his own ankle, found the odd hand that did not belong there, and shifted his grip to the alien wrist. And all the time he and the sea-thing were plunging deeper, the milky light growing dimmer.

The arm was long and furred, and powerful muscles were imbedded in a layer of fat. Stark's grip kept slipping, and he knew that if he lost it he was finished. He had been over-breathing while he swam, storing up oxygen; but he was using it at a great rate, and his heart was already hammering. His fingers clawed and tore, moving convulsively toward the point of leverage.

The smooth descent stopped. The creature turned its head and Stark saw the blurred face, eyes filmed and staring, bubbles trickling from a vestigial nose. The free arm that had been oaring them downward now swung over, not toward his hands but toward the back of his neck. The game was over.

Stark sunk his head between his shoulders. Talons ripped at the wet ridges of muscle. His own hand found a grip in a web of skin backing the creature's armpit. He straightened his body with a violent thrust and his ankle came free. He pulled himself under the creature's arm.

This Child of the Sea had also made a mistake. It had underestimated its victim. The humans who came its way, capsized fishermen or ritual offerings provided by the landbound worshippers of the Sea-Our-Mother, were easy prey. These poor souls knew they were doomed. Stark wasn't sure, and he had the thought of Ashton and the prophecy to bolster him. He managed to clamp his arms around the sinewy neck from behind, to lock his legs around the incredibly powerful body.

Then he hung on.

That in itself was a nightmare. The creature rolled and sounded, fighting to shake him off. It was like riding an angry whale, and Stark was dying, dying, tightening his hold in a blind red rage, determined not to die first.

When the sodden cracking of the neckbones came at last, he could hardly believe it.

He let go. The body fell away from him, dribbling dark bubbles from nose and mouth where the trapped breath vented. Stark went like an arrow for the surface.

Instinct made him break quietly. He hung there, savoring the deliciousness of fresh air in his lungs, trying not to sob audibly as he gulped it in. He could not at first remember why being absolutely quiet was imperative. Then, as the ringing darkness in his mind began to clear, he could hear again the laughing, hooting voices of the pack, waiting for their leader to bring them meat. And he knew that he dared not rest for long.

The battle had carried him beyond the narrow boat-channel, which was as well because he could not in any case go back to Skeg. The group on the cliff, like the Children, were still waiting. He could see them only as a dark blob in the distance, and he was sure they could not see him at all. With any luck, they might think he had perished in the sea.

With any luck. Stark smiled cynically. Not that he did not believe in luck. Rather, he had found it to be an uncertain ally.

With infinite caution, Stark swam the short distance to the shore and crawled out on dry land. There were ruins on the river bank here, a tangle of old walls long abandoned and overgrown with vines. They made excellent cover. Stark went in among them and then sat down, leaning his back against warm stone. Every joint and muscle was a separate anguish, bruised, strained, and clamoring.

A voice said, "Did you kill the thing?"

Stark looked up. A man stood in a gap in the wall, on the landward side. He had made no sound in coming there; it was as though he had been waiting for Stark's arrival and had only to move a handsbreadth. He wore a robe, and though the cluster-light altered colors, Stark was sure the robe was yellow.

"You're the man I saw at the ford."

"Yes. Gelmar and the girl came after you, and then a gang of Farers. The Farers threw stones at us and told us to go away. So we crossed back. I left my people and came down here to see what happened." He repeated, "Did you kill the thing?"

"I did."

"Then you'd better come away. They're not entirely seabound, you know. They'll be swarming here in a few minutes, hunting you." He added, "By the way, my name is Yarrod."

"Eric John Stark." He rose, suddenly aware that seaward the voices of the Children had fallen silent. Too much time had passed; they would know by now that something had gone wrong.

Yarrod set off through the ruins, and Stark followed until they had come what he thought to be a safe distance from the bar. Then he set his hand on Yarrod's shoulder and halted him.

"What have you to do with me, Yarrod?"

"I don't know yet." He studied Stark in the cluster-light. He was a tall man, wide in the shoulder, bony and muscular. Stark guessed that he was a warrior by trade, masquerading for some reason as something else. "Perhaps I'm curious to know why Gelmar would want to kill an off-worlder in a place where killing is forbidden even to the Farers."

From the sea there came a wild howling of grief and rage that set Stark's hackles bristling.

"Hear that?" said Yarrod. "They've found the body. Now Gelmar will know that you killed the thing, and he'll wonder whether or not you died also. He's bound to try and find out. Would you like to be hunted through these ruins by the Farers, or will you trust me to give you safe hiding?"

"I seem not to have much choice," said Stark, and shrugged. But he went warily behind Yarrod.

The tone of the howling changed as some of the creatures, from the distant sounds, began to clamber out onto the bar.

"What are they? Beast or human?"

"Both. A thousand or two years ago some people got the idea that the only salvation was for man to return to the Sea-Our-Mother, from whose womb we came. And they did it. They had their genes altered by some method that was still known then, to speed up the adaptation. And there they are, losing more of their humanness with every generation, and happier than we."

He increased his pace, and Stark matched it; the savage howling grew fainter in his ears. The consul might doubt the story that was told about the Children of the Sea; Stark did not. Not any more.

As though reading his thoughts, Yarrod chuckled. "Skaith is full of surprises. You've another one just ahead."

High on the bank above the ford of the river there was part of a barrel arch, intact overhead, open at both ends, which in that gentle climate scarcely mattered. Drooping vines acted as curtains. There was a fire burning inside, and the half dozen men and women Stark had seen before with Yarrod sat by it in a close group, heads together, arms intertwined. They neither moved nor looked up as Stark and Yarrod entered.

"Pretty good, aren't they?" said Yarrod. "Or do you know?"

Stark clawed back through his mental file on Skaith. "They're pretending to be a pod. And you're supposed to be a pod-master."

A pod, according to the file, was a collection of people so thoroughly sensitized by a species of group therapy that they no longer existed as individuals but only as interdependent parts of a single organism. The pod-master trained them, and then kept them fed and washed

and combed until such time as the hour arrived for To-
tal Fulfillment. That was when one of the components
died and the whole organism went, finding escape at
last. The average life of a pod was four years. Then the
pod-master started over again with another group.

"Pod-masters can go anywhere," said Yarrod.
"They're almost as holy as the Wandsmen." He turned
to the group. "All right, friends, you may breathe again,
but not for long. Gelmar and his rabble will be coming
soon, looking for our guest. Breca, go keep watch on the
ford, will you?"

The group broke up. A tall woman, evidently Breca,
went past them, giving Stark a strangely penetrating
look, and then vanished without a sound through the
vines. Stark studied the faces of the remaining five in
the firelight. They were strong faces, alert and wary, intensely curious, as though he might mean something to
them.

One of the five, a big man with a contentious air and
a jealous eye, whom Stark disliked on sight, asked Yarrod, "What was all that howling from the bar?"

Yarrod nodded at Stark. "He has killed a Child of the
Sea."

"And lived?" He sounded incredulous.

"I saw it," said Yarrod curtly. "Now tell us, Stark.
Why did Gelmar set the Farers on you?"

"Partly because I had been asking about Ashton. And
partly because of a prophecy."

Now they sighed sharply, as the Farer girl had.

"What prophecy?"

"Someone called Gerrith, the wise woman of Irnan,
prophesied that an off-worlder would come and destroy
the Lords Protector because of Ashton." He looked at
them shrewdly. "But you know all about that, don't
you?"

"We're all from Irnan," said Yarrod. "We waited and
waited, but Ashton never came, and then Gerrith made

her prophecy and the Wandsmen killed her. What was Ashton to you?"

"What is a father to a son, a brother to a brother?" Stark moved, easing the pains of his body, but there was no ease for the deeper pain, and they saw that and were disturbed. Stark's eyes held a lambent light.

"You people of Irnan decided to leave this planet, which I can readily understand. You applied through the GU consul at Skeg, keeping the matter very confidential, for help. The Ministry of Planetary Affairs agreed to find you a suitable place on another world and to supply the ships for your emigration. Ashton came to Skaith from the Ministry to discuss this with your leaders and make the final arrangements. As someone said, more fool he—because the whole thing had stopped being confidential. Who talked?"

"None of us," said Yarrod. "Perhaps someone at the consulate. Perhaps Ashton was clumsy."

"Gelmar took him on the Irnan road."

"Did Gelmar tell you that?"

"I don't think he meant to. He had other plans for me, and the information would have been breath wasted. So I took him with me into the sea and gave him a choice."

Yarrod groaned. "You took him into the sea. Don't you know that it is forbidden, absolutely forbidden on pain of death, to lay hands upon or interfere with a Wandsman in any way?"

"I was already under pain of death, and it seemed to me that in any case Gelmar needed a lesson in manners."

They stared at him. Then one of them laughed, and then they all laughed except the big man with the jealous eye who only showed his teeth. Yarrod said, "You may be the Dark Man at that."

The curtain of vines rustled faintly as Breca returned.

"There are people," she said, "coming to the ford. About twenty of them, and in a hurry."

4

Immediately the group fell silent. Yarrod began making swift gestures. "In here," he said in Stark's ear, and motioned to a fissure in the stonework at one side, barely large enough to accept a body the size of Stark's and of no size at all to permit any motion, offensive or defensive.

"Make up your mind," said Yarrod. "In a moment more we'll have to give you up to save ourselves."

Stark accepted the inevitable and slid himself into the crevice. The aperture was closed within seconds by the meager possessions of the Irnanese—leather bottles, sacks of meal and dried meat for the journey, a spare shift apiece—and by the pod itself, as the Irnanese formed their tight group beside the heap of dunnage. Stark had some difficulty breathing and he could not see anything, but he had been in worse places.

Provided the Irnanese did not sell him out. But he could not do much about that. He settled himself to endure.

From outside the vault he could hear no more than a muddy crowd sound. Then Gelmar entered the vault, and Stark could hear him quite clearly speaking to Yarrod.

"May your people have peace and quick Fulfillment, Master. I am Gelmar of Skeg."

Courtesy required that Yarrod should now identify himself in turn. He did so, giving a totally false name and place of origin and ending with a gravely unctuous, "What may I do for you, my son?"

"Has anyone passed this way? A man, an off-worlder, fresh from the sea, perhaps hurt?"

"No," said Yarrod, his voice steady and unconcerned. "I've seen no one. Besides, who escapes from the sea? I've heard the Children hunting within the hour."

"Perhaps the Master is lying," said a girl's voice spitefully, and Stark knew it well. "He was at the ford. He saw us."

"And your people threw stones at us," said Yarrod, sternly reproachful. "My pod became frightened, and it has cost me much effort to calm it. Even a Farer should have more respect."

"One must forgive them," said Gelmar. "They are the children of the Lords Protector. Do you lack for anything? Food? Wine?"

"There is enough. Perhaps tomorrow I shall come to Skeg and ask."

"It will be given gladly."

There were some parting formalities. Gelmar and the girl apparently left the vault, and in a moment Stark could hear whoops and cries as the Farers went haring away through the ruins.

Looking for me, Stark thought, and he was glad of his close crevice. A sorry rabble they were; but one against twenty, and the one unarmed, made for unpleasant odds.

For a time nothing happened except that Yarrod began to lead his pod in a kind of litany, a murmurous chant that almost put Stark to sleep. These people must have practiced well. There had to be a powerful reason to make them do it, and he thought he knew what it was.

The chanting faded gently to a small contented humming, and then Stark heard voices and sounds outside, returning.

Yarrod's voice came clearly. "You didn't find him?"

Rather distantly, Gelmar answered, "There was no sign. But the Children have been on the bar."

"No doubt they have already shared him, then."

"No doubt. Still, if you should see him . . . The man is a lawbreaker and dangerous. He laid hands on me and, being an off-worlder, he might not respect your robe."

"I have no fear, my son," said Yarrod, laying it on just a bit too much, Stark thought. "What do we all wish for but Fulfillment?"

"True," said Gelmar. "Good night, Master."

"Good night. And please to take your unruly flock with you. Each time the tranquillity of my pod is disturbed, the day of release is that much delayed."

Gelmar made some answer, and then there were more sounds, of people going away.

After what seemed a very long wait, Yarrod lifted aside the bundles. "Keep your voice down," he cautioned. "I think Gelmar left a few behind him. It's like trying to count vermin so I can't be sure, but I didn't see the girl."

Stark stood up and stretched. The pod had broken up again, and the woman Breca was missing, presumably on watch.

"Now then," said Yarrod brusquely, "we have a decision to make."

They all considered Stark.

"You believe that he is the Dark Man?" This was the big Irnanese who had spoken before with doubt.

"I think it likely. Gelmar appeared certain."

"But suppose he is not the Dark Man. Suppose we rush back to Irnan only to learn that. Then all our work is wasted and our mission is thrown away for nothing."

There were mutters of assent.

"That's possible, Halk. What do you suggest?"

"That we let him get to Irnan by himself. If he is truly the Dark Man, he'll make it."

"I don't particularly want to go to Irnan," said Stark, with a certain dangerous cheerfulness. "Ashton's not there."

"And well we know that," said Yarrod. "Where is he?"

"The Citadel of the Lords Protector, at Worldheart, wherever that is."

"North, in any case," said Yarrod. "And in any case, you must go to Irnan."

"Why?"

"So that Gerrith, the daughter of Gerrith, may say if you are truly the Dark Man of the prophecy."

"Oh. Gerrith had a daughter."

"All wise women have daughters if they can possibly manage it. Otherwise the precious genes are lost. And you see, Stark, we must know, or we cannot follow you. And without us and our help, you'll find it hard to do what you've come for."

"He'll find it hard anyway," said Halk, "but he might as well cooperate." He smiled at Stark. "You can't get away from Skaith now. Not through the starport. And there is no other way."

"I know that. Since I have no wish to leave, it scarcely matters, does it?" Stark turned to Yarrod. "Perhaps I can solve the immediate problem. Obviously you couldn't have come here to rescue me, so you must have had another reason. What was it?"

Yarrod fairly snarled. "We of Irnan are no longer allowed to travel without a special permit from the Wandsmen, and we didn't think they'd give us one for this journey. That's why we're flapping about in this silly disguise, so that we could come to Skeg and perhaps find out what the Galactic Union intends to do about us, if anything. I don't suppose they told you that at Pax? They seem to have told you everything else."

"As a matter of fact, they did."

The whole group moved a step closer.

"What will they do? Will they send someone?"

"They have sent someone," Stark said. "Me."

There was a sort of stunned silence. Then Halk asked, "Officially?" The sneer was audible.

"No. They've tried officially to reopen contact with Skaith, and got nowhere."

"So they sent you. Who is your master, then?"

Stark took Halk's meaning and grinned. "No one. I'm a mercenary by trade. Since I was coming anyway, the

Minister asked me to find out what I could about matters here and report to him—if I survived. I take no orders from him, and he takes no responsibility for me."

"Then," said Yarrod, "that is the best we can hope for?"

"Short of an invasion, yes. And the Galactic Union dislikes force. So if you want freedom you'll have to fight for it yourselves." Stark shrugged. "You must have realized that Skaith is not the most important planet in the galaxy."

"Except to us who live on it," said Yarrod. "Very well, then. We go back to Irnan. Agreed?"

Even Halk had to admit that, satisfactory or not, they had got what they came for.

"We mustn't go too quickly," said Yarrod, frowning. "That would give us away. Gelmar will expect me in Skeg tomorrow, and he'll surely keep some sort of watch on this side of the river."

Halk said, "What about Stark? We can hardly add him to the pod."

"He must go on ahead of us, tonight. He can wait at the—"

Breca came quickly through the vines, motioning for silence. "I hear them, coming this way."

"Stark—"

"Not in that hole again, thank you, though it was a good hole and welcome at the time. Did they search the roof?"

"They did." The pod began organizing itself, soundlessly and in haste.

"Then they'll likely not bother again." Stark went out through the rearward arch, letting the vines fall back quietly into place. He stood for a moment, head cocked. He could hear people moving about, some distance away. If they thought they were being stealthy they were much mistaken. The beautiful sky glowed with its islands of milky fire. In the cluster-light, Stark studied the broken masonry of the vault and then began to climb.

5

The top of the vault offered reasonable cover, with crumbling bits of wall still standing above the edges. Stark was not so much concerned now, since the main body of Farers had gone, but it would be wiser to avoid being seen.

He had no more than settled himself when Baya and two others came in view. Gelmar might have left them behind on purpose, after the search had failed, in the hope of catching somebody off guard. Or perhaps this scheme had been Baya's idea.

She was leading the other two, both men, who were obviously very bored and as pettish as babies. One was tall and spindly, totally naked except for body-paint that looked as if he had rolled in it. His hair and beard were full of rubbish. The other man was shorter and fatter, and that was all Stark could see of him because he was completely wrapped about with lengths of bright cloth that covered even his face. The folds were stuck full of flowers.

"Let's go back now, Baya," said the tall one, turning toward the ford. "You've seen there's no one here."

"The Dark Man died in the sea," said the shorter one, his voice squeaking impatiently through his veils. "The Children shared him. How could it be otherwise?"

Baya lifted her shoulders as though a breath of cold air had touched her. She shook her head.

"I spoke to him," she said. "I touched him. There was something about him. Strength, a terrible strength. He killed a Child of the Sea, remember?"

"You're being silly," said the short one, and hopped

up and down like a rabbit. "Girl-silly. You saw his muscles, and you want him to be alive. You're sorry he
didn't love you before he died."

"Hold your tongue," said Baya. "Maybe he's dead,
and maybe he isn't, and if he isn't, someone is hiding
him. Stop whining and look around."

"But we've already searched——"

The rubbishy one sighed. "We'd better do as she says,
I suppose. You know what a terrible temper she has."

They wandered off, out of Stark's sight but not out of
his hearing. Baya continued to stand where she was,
frowning at the flickerings of firelight that shone from
the vault. Then she sauntered over, her insolent body
agleam in the light of the Three Ladies. Stark lost sight
of her, too, since she was directly beneath him, but he
could hear the vines rustle as she swept them aside.

"Master . . . "

Yarrod's angry voice sounded from the vault. "You
have no business here. Get out."

"But, Master, I'm only curious," said Baya. "I might
even want to join a pod myself one day, when I'm tired
of being a Farer. Tell me about them, Master. Is it true
that they forget about everything, even love?"

The vines swished as she entered the vault and let
them fall behind her.

The voices from within were now too muffled for
Stark to understand the words. In a very few minutes a
squeal of pain came from Baya, and the vines thrashed
wildly as she and Yarrod came through them. Yarrod
had his hand wound cruelly in her hair, and he marched
her, crying and struggling, away from the vault. He took
her to the river bank and pushed her in.

"You've done enough mischief for one day," he said.
"If you come near my pod again, I'll make you regret
it." And he spat, and added, "Farer trash! I have no
need of you."

He left her and strode back to the vault. She stood in

the shallow water of the ford and shook her fists at him, screaming.

"You live on the bounty of the Lords Protector just the same as we do! What makes you so much better, you—" She poured out obscenities, then choked on her own rage and ended up coughing.

There was a sudden delighted outcry from among the ruins where her two companions were poking around. She came up the bank.

"Have you found him?"

"We found love-weed! Love-weed!" The two Farers reappeared, waving handsful of something they had grubbed up, chewing greedily. The tall one held some out to Baya.

"Here. Forget the dead man. Let us love and enjoy."

"No. I don't feel like loving now." She turned away, toward the vault. "I feel like hating. Pod-masters are supposed to be holy men. This one is too full of hate."

"Perhaps it's because we threw stones," said the short one, cramming his mouth full.

"Who cares?" said the tall one, and grabbed Baya by the shoulder. "Eat this, and you'll feel like loving." He pushed some of the weed by main force into Baya's mouth.

She spat it out. "No! I must talk to Gelmar. I think there's something—"

"Later," said the Farer. "Later." He laughed, and the short one laughed, and they shoved Baya back and forth between them. The struggle seemed to pleasure them, and hasten the action of the drug. Baya pulled the bodkin from her hair. She slashed the naked one once, not deeply, and they laughed some more and took the bodkin away from her. Then they worried her down to the ground and began beating her.

The roof of the vault was not high. Stark came down off it in one jump. The Farers neither heard nor saw him. They were far too busy, and Baya was screaming at the top of her lungs. Stark hit the tall one a chopping blow at the base of the skull and he fell, and the shorter one followed him without a groan, strewing the last of his flowers. Stark heaved the bodies aside. Baya looked up at him, her eyes wide and dazed. She said something, perhaps his name. He could not be sure. He found the nerve-center in the side of her neck and pressed it; she was quiet.

He saw that Yarrod had come out and was standing over him, looking like thunder.

"That was ill-done," said Yarrod. "You fool, who cares what happens to a Farer?"

"You're the fool," said Stark. "You gave yourself away. She was going to tell Gelmar that the pod-master was a fraud." He lifted the girl smoothly to his shoulder and stood up.

"She saw you, I suppose."

"I think so."

"And these?"

The two men had begun to snore heavily. They smelled of a sweet-sour pungency. Their mouths were open and smiling.

"No," said Stark. "But they heard Baya. About you, I mean. They may remember."

"All right," said Yarrod, still angry. "I suppose it makes no difference who's to blame. The only choice we have now is to run, and run fast."

He looked across the river to the lights of Skeg and then went stamping back to the vault.

Within minutes they were on their way, through the sprawling ruins and into the jungle. The Three Ladies smiled serenely. The warm air was moist, heavy with the smells of night-flowering creepers, mud, and decay. Nameless things scuttled and clicked, bickering in tiny voices round their feet. Stark adjusted Baya's light weight more comfortably across his shoulders.

"The roads are closed to off-worlders," he said. "I suppose you've thought of that."

"You don't imagine we came here by the road, do

you?" Yarrod said. "We got out of Irnan by pretending to be a hunting party. We left our mounts and all our proper gear at a place on the other side of the hills and walked in, by a jungle path." He squinted at the sky. "We can be there by tomorrow noon, if we kill ourselves."

"There's a chance, isn't there," said Stark, "that Gelmar will think you've moved your people out because of the disturbance? And that Baya simply ran off? She stabbed one of her friends, you know, and her knife is still there."

"Of course there's a chance. He can't be sure of anything, can he? He can't even be sure whether you're dead or alive. So if you were Gelmar, what would you do?"

"I'd send word along to be on watch, especially to Irnan." And he cursed the name of Gerrith, wishing that she had kept her mouth shut.

"She got her death by it," said Yarrod curtly. "That should be punishment enough."

"It's my death that I'm like to get by it that worries me," said Stark. "If I'd known about the damned prophecy, I'd have laid my plans differently."

"Well," said Halk, smiling his fleeting smile at Stark, "if it's a true prophecy, and you are a fated man, you have nothing to fear, have you?"

"The man who doesn't fear, doesn't live long. I fear everything." He patted Baya's bare thigh. "Even this."

"In that, you're well-advised. You'd do best to kill it."

"We'll see," said Stark. "No need to hurry."

They moved on, following a little still green star that Yarrod called the Lamp of the North.

"If Gelmar does send word to Irnan, he'll do it in the usual manner, by messenger, by the roads. Barring accident, we should be well ahead."

"If," said Halk, "the Dark Man and his baggage don't slow us down."

Stark showed the edges of his teeth. "Halk," he said, "I have a feeling that you and I are not going to be the best of friends."

"Bear with him, Stark," said Yarrod. "He's a fighter, and we need swords more than we need sweet tempers."

That at least was true. Stark saved his breath for walking. And there was plenty of that for all of them.

6

It was daybreak and they had stopped to rest, high on the shoulder of a jungle hill. The dreaming sea lay far behind them, all its deadliness hidden by distance and morning mists that took fantastic colors from the rising of the ginger star. The Irnanese faced eastward and each one poured a small libation. Even Baya bowed her head.

"Hail, Old Sun, we thank you for this day," they muttered, and sounded as though they meant it. Then Halk, as usual, spoiled the effect. He turned defiantly to Stark.

"We were not always paupers, hoarding our little daylight, grudging every scrap of metal so that we can still have a knife to cut our meat. There were ships on that sea. There were machines that flew in the air, and all manner of things that are only legend now. Skaith was a rich world once, as rich as any."

"It lived too long," said Yarrod. "It's senile and mad, growing madder with every generation. Come and eat."

They sat down and began sharing meager rations of food and sour wine. When it was Baya's turn they passed her by.

Stark asked, "Is there none for the girl?"

"We've been feeding her and the likes of her all our lives," said Breca. "She can do without."

"Besides," said Halk, "we didn't ask her to come."

Stark divided his own ration and gave her half. She took it and ate it quickly, saying nothing. She had been docile enough since she regained consciousness, going on her own feet with only a small amout of whimpering, Stark leading her like a puppy with a halter round her neck. He knew she was afraid, surrounded by people

34

who made no secret of their hatred and with no protective Wandsman at hand to whip them into line. Her eyes were large and hollow and her body-paint was a sorry mess, all sweated and smeared.

"The old civilizations," said Yarrod, around a flap of tough bread, "for all their technology, never achieved space-flight. I suppose they were busy with more important things. So there was no escape, for them or for us. No hope of escape. And then suddenly there was talk that starships had landed, talk about a Galactic Union and about other worlds; you see what that did to us when we knew it was true. There was hope. We could escape."

Stark nodded. "I can see also why the Wandsmen would be unhappy about the idea. If the providers start leaving, their whole system collapses."

Halk leaned toward Baya. "And it will collapse. And what will you do then, little Farer girl? Eh?"

She shrank away from him, but he kept on at her until he brought her deep anger flaring up.

"It'll never happen," she snarled at him. "The Protectors won't let it. They'll hunt you all down and kill you." She looked hatefully at Stark. "Off-worlders have no business here, making trouble. They should never have been allowed to come."

"But they did come," said Stark, "and things will never be the same again." He smiled at Baya. "If I were you I'd start thinking about learning to scratch for myself. And of course, you could always emigrate."

"Emigrate," said Halk. "Ha! Then she would have to do more than just love and enjoy."

"Skaith is dying," said Baya. "What else is there to do?"

Stark shook his head. "Skaith will last out your lifetime, and one or two more. So that's not much of a reason."

She cursed him and began to cry furiously. "You're wicked, you're all wicked, you'll all die just like that woman Gerrith. The Lords Protector will punish you. They defend the weak, they feed the hungry, they shelter the—"

"You can keep that," said Halk, and he cuffed her. She shut up, but her eyes still smoldered. Halk lifted his hand again.

"Let her be," said Stark. "She didn't invent the system." He turned to Yarrod. "If Irnan is as closely watched as you say, how shall I get in and out of the city without being seen?"

"You won't have to. The wise woman's grotto is in the foothills, at the head of the valley."

"Don't they watch her, too?"

"Like hawks." And he added grimly, "We can handle that."

Halk was still looking at Baya, full of malice. "What will you do with her?"

"Turn her loose, when her tongue can do us no harm."

"When will that be? No, give her to me, Dark Man. I'll see to it that she's harmless."

"No."

"Why the tender care for her life? She was ready enough to help take yours."

"She has reason to hate and fear me." Stark looked at Baya's tear-stained face and smiled again. "Besides, she was acting only from the noblest motives."

"Hell," said Yarrod, "who isn't?"

When they had eaten they started on again, pushing themselves almost to the limit of endurance, which meant far past Baya's limit. Stark carried her part of the time, staggering a little with weariness himself and fully conscious of every ache bequeathed to him by the late Child of the Sea. They climbed, and the ginger star climbed above them. About midmorning they crossed the ridge and began going down, which was easier at first and then harder as the grade became steeper. The dim path switched back and forth across the face of the slope, but in many places Yarrod led them straight down in order to save time.

They did not quite kill themselves. They did not quite reach the place they were heading for by noon, either. Stark judged that Old Sun was at least an hour past his zenith when Yarrod at last signaled a halt.

They were in a dense grove of trees, with pale trunks all grooved and ridged and dark foliage high above that shut out the sky. Moving cautiously, Yarrod started on again. Halk went with him. Stark handed Baya's leash to Breca and joined them. The Irnanese were expert woodsmen, he noticed, and yet his ears winced at the noise they made. When they reached the edge of the grove they became even more careful, peering out from behind the trees.

Stark saw a broad sunny meadow. There was a ruined tower some distance along it that might once have been a mill or part of a fortified dwelling. Two men in bright tunics and leather jerkins sat in the doorway of the tower, relaxed and at ease, their weapons leaned beside them. It was too far away to see their faces. Scattered about between the grove and the tower, a dozen or so big shaggy rusty-brown animals fed contentedly on lush grass. There were no sounds except the natural ones; breezes rustling overhead, animals cropping.

Yarrod was satisfied. He had expected no less. He turned to call the others on.

And Stark caught his shoulder in a grip of iron. "Wait!"

Where a moment ago there had been no sounds, now all at once there were a multitude.

"Men. There. And there—"

It was plain for all to hear—the creak of sandal-leather, the clink of metal, the swift stealthy motion.

"All around us, closing in—"

Yarrod shouted. The Irnanese, aware that they were in a trap, began to run. Baya stumbled and fell, or perhaps deliberately lay down. At any rate, they left her.

Voices called out with peremptory orders to halt. There was a loud trampling of feet. The Irnanese fled across the meadow, toward the tower where their weapons were. Arrows flew, whickering in the bright air. Two Irnanese fell, and only one got up again. They dodged in and out among the grazing animals that snorted and lumbered aside. Then Stark saw that the men in the doorway had not moved, and he knew they were dead.

The meadow was wide, wide and naked in the sunlight, and now a flight of arrows came from the tower and stuck quivering in the ground around them.

Yarrod stopped. He looked from side to side, but there was no hiding place, no hope. Men were coming out of the grove behind them, arrows nocked. More men came out of the tower, kicking the bodies aside. A small rufous man led them. He wore a dark red tunic and carried no weapon but his wand of office. Halk said one word, a name, and he said it like a curse.

"Mordach!"

Stark had made his own decision. Those arrows were long and sharp, and he was sure that he could not outrun them. So he, too, stood and waited, having no wish to die in this meaningless place under the ginger star.

"Who is Mordach?" he asked.

"Chief Wandsman of Irnan," said Yarrod, his voice breaking with rage and despair. "Someone talked; someone betrayed us."

The men formed a wall around them, and Mordach came through that wall to stand smiling up at the tall Irnanese.

"The hunting party," he said. "In strange attire, and without weapons. Yet I see that you did find game of a sort." His gaze fastened on Stark, and Stark thought that perhaps he ought to have chanced the arrows after all.

"An off-worlder," said Mordach, "where off-worlders are forbidden to be. And traveling with a company of lawbreakers. Was this what you went to find? Someone who could pretend to fulfill your prophecy?"

"Perhaps he does fulfill it, Mordach," said Halk wickedly. "Gelmar thought so. He tried to kill him, and could not."

Thank you, friend, thought Stark, and felt his guts tighten in anticipation.

Two men came up supporting Baya between them. "We found her in the grove. She doesn't look to be one of them."

"I'm a Farer," said Baya, and went on her knees to Mordach. "In the name of the Lords Protector—" She held out the end of the halter and shook it. "He took me by force, away from Skeg."

"He?"

"That man. The off-worlder. Eric John Stark."

"Why?"

"Because he lived when he ought to have died." She looked up at Stark, trembling with malevolence. "He escaped from us, into the sea. You know what that means, but he lived. He killed a Child of the Sea, and lived. And I saw him." If she had had strength and breath left she would have screamed, "He is the Dark Man of the prophecy! Kill him! Kill him now!"

"There," said Mordach absently, and caressed her tangled hair. He considered Stark, his eyes hooded and cold. "So. And perhaps even Gelmar could be mistaken. Either way—"

"Kill him," Baya whimpered. "Please. Now."

"Killing is a solemn matter," Mordach said, "and salutary. It ought not to be wasted." He motioned to some of his men. "Bind them. Securely, very securely, and especially the off-worlder." He lifted Baya to her feet. "Come, child, you're safe now."

"Mordach," said Yarrod. "Who betrayed us?"

"You did," said Mordach. "Yourselves. All your preparations took time and effort, and some of them were observed. You and Halk are known to be among the most active of the Emigration Party; the others were known to be associates. When you all went off together to hunt, we were curious to know what the quarry might be. So we followed. After we came here to the tower, we only had to wait." His gaze wandered again to Stark. "You were bringing him back to Gerrith's daughter, weren't you?"

Yarrod did not answer, but Mordach nodded. "Of course you were. And of course they must meet, and I promise you they shall—openly, where all can see."

He went off with Baya, who looked back once over her shoulder as the men-at-arms moved in with leather thongs and began to bind the captives. They were neither rough nor gentle, merely very efficient. They were of a type Stark had not seen before, having lint-white hair and sharply slanted cheekbones and slitted yellow eyes that gave them the look of wolves. They were certainly not Farers.

"Farers are only a mob, for trampling and tearing," Yarrod said. "Wandsmen in the city-states like to have a small force of mercenaries for the serious work, and they recruit them along the Border. These are from Izvand, in the Inner Barrens." His head hung down in shame and misery, but he lifted it fiercely when one of the mercenaries brought a halter for his neck, so that he might take the rope easily and with a semblance of pride. "I'm sorry," he said, and would not meet Stark's eye.

And now it was Stark's turn to wear a halter round his own neck, and to walk behind in the dust while Baya rode.

So at length the Dark Man came to Irnan.

7

It was a gray city, walled in stone and set on a height roughly in the center of a broad valley that was green with spring. Mordach and his prisoners and his mercenaries had journeyed a long way north, and a long way up over rainy mountains, and they had left the tropical summer far behind. All around Irnan were tilled fields and pastures and orchards in blossom, a froth of pink and white oddly tarnished by the light of the ginger star.

A road led to the city. There was much traffic on it: farm carts, people going to and from their work in the fields or driving beasts before them, traders and long strings of pack-animals jingling with bells, a troop of mountebanks, a caravan of traveling whores of both sexes with bright banners advertising their wares, and the motley assortment of wanderers that seemed to be omnipresent on Skaith. Mordach's party went down the middle of the road, four men-at-arms riding in front and clashing short stabbing spears rhythmically against their shields. A clear way was made for them, and behind them the people stood along the roadside ditches and stared and pointed and whispered, and then began to follow.

Two Wandsmen, in green tunics that indicated their lesser rank, came out of the gate to meet Mordach, with a rabble of Farers at their heels. And within minutes, the word was running ahead like wildfire.

"The Dark Man! They've taken the Dark Man! They've taken the traitors!"

More Wandsmen appeared as though from between the paving stones. A crowd gathered, clotting round Mordach's party like swarming bees. The mercenaries

41

drew their ranks tighter, until their mounts all but trod upon the captives, and their spears pointed outward, forming a barrier against the press of bodies.

"Keep up, keep up," said the captain of the Izvandians. "If you fall, we can't help you."

They passed beneath the arch of the great gate. Stark saw that the stone was stained and weathered, the carvings grown dim with time. A winged creature with a sword in its claws crouched on the capstone, fierce jaws open to bite the world. The valves of the gate were very strong, sheathed in cured hides almost as hard as metal. There was a passage through the thickness of the wall, a sort of dark tunnel where every sound was caught and compressed and the din of voices was stunning. Then they were in the square beyond and forcing their way between market stalls, toward a central platform built stoutly of wood and higher than the jostling heads of the mob. Some of the mercenaries stood guard while others dismounted and hurried the captives up a flight of steps. Stark guessed that the square was the only open space of any size within the walls and that the platform was used for all public occasions such as executions and other edifying entertainments.

There were standing posts, permanently placed and black with use. Within moments Stark and Yarrod and the others were bound to them. The mercenaries took up stations at the edges of the platform, facing outward. The two Wandsmen in green went away; apparently Mordach had sent them on some errand. Mordach himself addressed the crowd. Much of what he said was drowned in an animal howling, but there was little doubt about the burden of his speech. Irnan had sinned, and those who were guilty were about to pay.

Stark flexed himself against the hide ropes. They cut his flesh but did not give. The post was firm as a tree. He leaned back against it, easing himself as much as possible, and looked at this place where presumably he was about to die.

"What do you think now, Dark Man?" asked Halk.

He was bound to the post on Stark's left, Yarrod on his right.

"I think," said Stark, "that we'll soon know whether Gerrith had the true sight."

And once more he cursed the name of Gerrith, but this time he kept it to himself.

The crowd was still growing. People came until it seemed that the space could not hold any more, and still they came. Around the inner sides of the square there were buildings of stone, narrow and high, shouldering together, slate roofs peaked and shining in the sun. The upper windows were filled with people looking down. After a while folk were straddling the rooftrees and perching on the gutters, and the tops of the outer walls were packed.

Two distinct elements were in the crowd, and they seemed not to mingle. Foremost round the platform, doing all the screaming, were the Farers and the other flotsam. Beyond them, and quite quiet, were the people of Irnan.

"Any hope from them?" asked Stark.

Yarrod tried to shrug. "Not all of them are with us. Our people have lived in this place a long time, and the roots go deep. And Skaith, with all its faults, is the only world we know. Some folk find the idea of leaving it frightening to the point of blasphemy, and they won't lift a hand to help us. About the others, I'm not making any bets."

Mordach was urging the mob to be patient; more things were to come. Still they pushed and clamored for blood. A band of women forced their way to the steps and began to climb. They wore black bags over their heads, covering their faces. Otherwise they were naked and their skin was like tree-bark from long exposure.

"Give us the Dark Man, Mordach!" they cried. "Let us take him to the mountain top and feed his strength to Old Sun!"

Mordach held up his staff to halt them. He spoke to them gently, and Stark asked, "What are they?"

"They live wild in the mountains. Once in a while, when they get hungry, they come in. They worship the sun, and any man they can manage to capture they sacrifice. They believe that they alone keep Old Sun alive." Halk laughed. "Look at the greedy beasts! They'd like to have all of us."

Arms like gnarled branches reached and clawed.

"They will die, little sisters," said Mordach. "They will all feed Old Sun, and you shall watch and sing the Hymn of Life."

Gently he urged them back, and reluctantly they returned to the crowd. All at once Stark heard a shouting and a turmoil about the doors of one of the buildings overlooking the square, and a procession moved out from it with the green Wandsmen leading and a fringe of Farers flapping at the sides and rear. At the center, Stark made out a dozen or so men and women in sober gowns, with chains of office round their necks. They walked in an odd manner, and as they came closer he could see that they were bound in such a way as forced them to bend forward and shuffle like penitents.

A low deep groan came from the people of Irnan, and Yarrod said between his teeth, "Our chiefs and elders."

Stark thought he saw the beginning of movement among the Irnanese, and he hoped they would rush the crowd and rescue their leaders by force, starting a general revolt. The movement rippled and died. The procession came to the steps and climbed haltingly while the mob jeered. The elders were herded onto the platform and made to stand, and Mordach pointed his staff at them in a gesture of wrath and accusation.

"You have done wickedness," he cried, in a voice that rang across the square. "Now you shall do penance!"

The crowd screamed. They threw things. The citizens of Irnan stirred uneasily. They muttered, but still they did not move.

"They're afraid," Yarrod said. "The Wandsmen have packed the town with Farers, as you see. One word, and they'll start tearing Irnan apart stone by stone."

"Still, the Irnanese outnumber them."

"Our party does not. And the Wandsmen have hostages." He nodded his red head at the men and women standing bent in the sun.

There was a smell in the air now. The hot, close, frightening smell of mob; mob excited, hungry, dreaming blood and death. The primitive in Stark knew that sweaty acridity all too well. The ropes cut him; the post was hard against his back. The ginger star burned him with brassy light and his own sweat ran down.

Someone shouted, "Where is the wise woman?"

Other voices took up the cry, howled it back and forth between the gray walls.

"Where is the wise woman? Where is Gerrith?"

Mordach calmed them. "She has been sent for. She will be with us soon."

Yarrod cursed Mordach. "Do you plan to murder her as you did her mother?"

Mordach only smiled and said, "Wait."

They waited. The crowd became increasingly restless. Roving bands began looting the market stalls, scattering food and produce, smashing the stalls themselves to make clubs. Wine and drugs passed freely. Stark wondered how much longer Mordach could hold them.

Then the cry went up from the gate. "The wise woman! Gerrith is coming!"

An expectant quiet settled over the square. The hundreds of heads turned, and it seemed as though the Irnanese all drew one deep breath and held it.

Men-at-arms appeared, clearing a way through the press. Behind them came a cart, a farm cart soiled and reeking with the work of the fields, and after that more men-at-arms bringing up the rear.

Inside the cart were two Wandsmen, each one clinging with one hand to the jolting stakes and holding with the other the tall figure of a woman who stood between them.

8

She was dressed all in black, in a great veil that envel-
oped her from head to heels, a single shroud-like gar-
ment that concealed her face and all else beside her
height. Set upon her head and circling the veil was a
diadem the color of old ivory.

"The Robe and Crown of Fate," said Yarrod, and
the folk of Irnan let out that held breath in a savage wail
of protest.

The mob drowned it in their own blood-cry.

Men-at-arms and farm cart crossed the square, halted
at the platform steps. The woman was made to leave the
cart and climb. The diadem appeared first above the
level of the floor. It looked very frail and old, and its ornament was a circle of little grinning skulls. Then there
was the sway of dark draperies, and Gerrith, the wise
woman of Irnan, stood before Mordach with the Wandsmen on either side.

Because of the veil Stark could not be sure, but he
thought that Gerrith was looking past Mordach, straight
at him.

Yet she spoke to Mordach, and her voice was clear
and sweet and ringing, without a hint of fear.

"This was not well done, Mordach."

"No?" he said. "Let us see." He turned from her,
speaking over the heads of his Farers to the people of
Irnan. His voice carried to the walls. "You of Irnan!
Watch now, and learn!"

He turned again to Gerrith and pointed his wand at
Stark. "What do you see there, daughter of Gerrith?"

"I see the Dark Man."

46

"The Dark Man of your mother's prophecy?"

"Yes."

Well, thought Stark, and what else could she say?

"The Dark Man, bound and helpless, waiting for death." Mordach laughed. He laughed often, as though he found these human lapses from reason genuinely amusing. "He will destroy nothing. Do you recant, woman? Do you admit the lie?"

"No."

"Then you are no wiser than your mother, and your sight is no more true. Do you hear out there, you of Irnan?" Again his words carried far, and where they did not reach other tongues took them up and passed them on, whispering like surf against the walls, up to the windows and the rooftops. "Your prophecy is false, your wise woman a liar, your Dark Man a sham!"

In one swift motion he ripped crown and veil from Gerrith.

Astonishment, surprise, shock, outrage! Stark could hear the sounds beyond the delighted screaming of the mob. Halk, Yarrod, and the other Irnanese on the platform made instinctive, futile movements toward the killing of Mordach.

Only Gerrith stood tall and calm, as though she had expected this. As indeed she must have done, thought Stark, unless the wise women of Irnan habitually went naked beneath the ceremonial veil. And naked she was, all warm bronze with the sunlight on her and a thick braid of bronzy hair hanging down her back. Her body was strong and straight and proud, not flinching before the lewdness of the crowd. Nudity was commonplace on Skaith and hardly to be noticed, but this was different. This act was a stripping of more than the mere body. Mordach was attempting to strip her soul.

He tossed the black veil out to the mob and let them tear it. The diadem he smashed beneath his feet and kicked the old yellowed fragments contemptuously away.

"There are your robe and crown," he said. "We will have no more wise women at Irnan."

This, too, she had expected. But her eyes held a cold and terrible light.

"And you will have no more Irnan to rob, Mordach." She spoke with the tongue of prophecy, and it made Stark shiver with its finality. "The Crown has come with us from the old Irnan, all through the Great Wandering and the centuries of rebuilding. Now you have destroyed it, and the history of Irnan is finished."

Mordach shrugged and said, "Bind her."

But before the men-at-arms could reach her she turned and raised her arms and cried out in that wonderful ringing voice.

"Irnan is finished. You must go and build a new city, on a new world."

Then she submitted herself to the binding, and Mordach said, "Do not go at once, people of Irnan! Stay a while and watch the Dark Man die."

A roar of laughter swept the crowd. "Yes, stay!" they jeered. "Don't leave us now. At least wait for the ships to come."

Yarrod, bound to his post, threw back his head and screamed a harsh wild scream.

"Rise up, you dogs! Rise up and tear them! Where are your guts, your pride, your manhood—"

The madness was on him, the madness that makes dead men and heroes. Mordach lifted his hand. One of the Izvandians stepped up and quite impersonally thrust his short spear into Yarrod's breast. A clean and merciful stroke, Stark noticed, though he was sure Mordach would have preferred something more lingering. Yarrod fell silent and sagged against the post.

"Cut him down," said Mordach. "Throw his body to the crowd."

The tree-bark women commenced a shrill chanting, raising their arms to the sun.

Yarrod's red head, cometlike, marked his passage.

Stark preferred not to watch what happened after that, though he could not shut out the sounds. He lifted his gaze to the walls of Irnan, the windows and the roof-tops, peripherally aware that Gerrith was brought and bound to the post that Yarrod had just quitted.

Amazingly, at his other side, Halk had begun to weep.

Mordach and the other Wandsmen stood benignly watching their flock, talking among themselves, planning the next act, the dramatic climax of their lecture on the folly of rebellion. In the background, many of the Irnanese were going. They had their cloaks pulled over their heads, as though they could not bear any more. They melted away into the narrow streets around the square.

Gerrith was speaking. "So they leave us," she said. Stark turned his attention to her. She was looking at him. Her eyes were a warm gold-bronze in color—very honest eyes, sorrowful but calm.

"It seems that Mordach is right, that Gerrith's proph-ecy was born of her own desires and not the true sight. So you will die for nothing and that is a great pity." She shook her head. The bronze braid had fallen forward over her shoulder and the shining end of it moved be-tween her breasts. "A great pity." She studied him, his size and strength, the structure of his facial bones, the shape of his mouth, the expression of his eyes. She seemed full of regret and compassion. "I'm sorry. Why did you come here?"

"Looking for Ashton."

She seemed astounded. "But—"

"But that's what Gerrith said, isn't it? So perhaps, af-ter all—"

She would have spoken again but he cautioned her to silence. The wandsmen were still talking. The men-at-arms had returned to their positions, looking disdainfully at the mob that growled and howled and bestially tore. Stark glanced again at the windows.

Perhaps he was imagining—

The windows were no longer crowded with watchers. They were empty, and shutters were being pulled to but not closed, as though to hide what went on in the rooms behind them and yet leave a view of the square. There were still people on the roofs but not so many, and there seemed to be movement of a furtive sort behind turrets and chimney-stacks. Stark took a deep breath and allowed himself a very small bit of hope.

The thing was to be ready if it happened.

Mordach came and stood before him. "Well," he said, "and how shall the Dark Man die? Shall I give him to the Little Sisters of the Sun? Shall I let my Farers play with him? Or shall I have him flayed?" The tip of his wand traced lines on Stark's skin. "Slowly, of course. A strip at a time. Yes. And whom shall we call to flay our Dark Man? The Izvandians? No, this is not their affair." He looked at the Irnanese elders standing bowed in their shackles. "It is *their* affair. *They* planned to desert us, to deny their duty to their fellow men. *They* fell into the error of selfishness and greed. The Dark Man is their symbol. *They* shall flay him!"

The crowd was overjoyed.

Mordach took a dagger from his belt and thrust it into the hand of a graybeard, who stared back at him with loathing and dropped it.

Mordach smiled. "I haven't given the alternative, old man. The choice is simple. A strip of his skin, or your life."

"Then," said the graybeard, "I must die."

"As you wish," said Mordach. He turned toward the nearest man-at-arms, one hand uplifted, his mouth open to speak.

Stark heard the ripping thud of the arrow into flesh, saw the feathered butt rise out of Mordach's breast as though it had suddenly blossomed there. Mordach drew in one shocked breath, a kind of inverted scream. He looked up and saw all the shuttered windows opening and the men with bows standing in them, and the shafts beginning to pour down like hissing rain, and then he went to his knees and watched his Izvandians and his green Wandsmen drop; and he turned his face to Stark and the wise woman with the beginning of a horrible doubt. Stark was glad that Mordach had that to take with him into the dark.

The graybeard had been a warrior in his time. He touched Mordach's body with his foot and said fiercely, "Perhaps there's hope for us after all."

More archers appeared, on the walls, on the roofs. They were shooting into the mob now. There was a great squalling and shrieking, a surge of panic this way and that as the entertainment ceased to be fun.

Stark saw a body of mercenaries come in from the gate. At the same time, from the side streets, the citizens of Irnan began to stream into the square, armed with anything they could get their hands on. Among them was one group, well armed and keeping close order. These men cut their way through the pack with ruthless efficiency, heading for the platform. They gained it. A few of them stayed to hold the steps. The others hustled the elders down and cut the captives loose. Stark and the survivors of Yarrod's band caught up weapons from the dead Izvandians. They went down the steps and closed ranks around Gerrith and the elders. They started to fight their way back into the streets.

Some of the Farers, crazy with drugs and fanatic hatred, rushed the group, careless of the swords. The Irnanese cried, "Yarrod! Yarrod!" They killed their way across the square to the rhythm of their savage, bitter chant.

They passed into a narrow street between buildings of gray stone that had grown up during the centuries and then grown together overhead, so that in some places the street was more like a tunnel. It was quiet here. They hurried on, as rapidly as the elders could move, and presently entered a doorway. Beyond it was a hall of some size, hung with banners and furnished with one great table and a row of massive chairs. Some people were gathered there. Immediately they took the elders and helped them to the chairs, and one man shouted,

"Armorer! Come here and get these shackles off!"

Someone had brought a cloak to Gerrith and covered her. She was standing beside Stark. She turned to him with a fey look and said,

"Now, indeed, I believe."

9

Halk spoke. His eyes were red with rage and weeping but his mouth smiled, all teeth and vengefulness.

"They don't need us here, Dark Man. Are you coming?"

Gerrith nodded. "Go if you will, Stark. Your bane is not in Irnan."

He wondered if she knew of another place where it would be.

He went back into the streets with Halk. Little bands of citizens were hunting Farers down like rabbits in the twists and turns of the narrow ways. Obviously the Irnanese had matters firmly in hand. In the square, archers were taking up new positions around the gate, where scores of Farers were shrieking and trampling one another, fighting to get out and away. Stark saw no sign of the Izvandians. With their paymaster dead, he guessed they had simply retired into their barracks and let the battle go on without them. The tree-bark women had taken refuge underneath the platform, more to escape the crush, apparently, then because they were afraid. They were chanting ecstatically, busy with the task of feeding Old Sun. The ginger star was feasting well today.

There was really not much left to do. A few last pockets of resistance, some mopping up of strays, but the fight was won, had been won, really, with that first flight of arrows. Mordach's body still lay on the platform. The little man had pushed too hard. Even the folk whom Yarrod had said would not lift a hand to save them had lifted both hands to save their elders and their wise woman and to cleanse themselves of the shame Mordach had put upon them.

Stark let Halk go on alone to exact more payment for Yarrod. He couldn't see that he was needed anywhere, so he put up his sword and climbed to the platform. Among the sprawled bodies he found the fragments of old ivory where Mordach had trampled the crown. Only one of the little skulls was still intact, grinning as though it could taste the blood that speckled it. He picked it up and went down the steps again, with the voices of the tree-bark women shrill in his ears. He hoped that he would never meet a pack of them baying on their own mountain-tops. He found his way through the streets, back to the council hall.

There was a bustle of messengers, people coming and going, a feeling of urgency. Stark did not see Gerrith, so he put the small skull away in the rags of his tunic. He was standing wondering what to do next when a man came up to him and said,

"Jerann asks that you come with me."

"Jerann?"

The man indicated Graybeard. "The chief of our Council. I am to see that you have everything you need."

Stark thanked the man and followed him along a corridor and up a winding stair to another corridor and into a chamber with narrow windows set in the thickness of the stone walls. A fire burned on the hearth. There was a bed, a chest, a settle, all heavy and well made, and a rug of coarse wool on the floor. Opening off the chamber was a bathroom with a little stone bath reached by three steps. Serving men waited with pails of steaming water and rough towels. Gratefully Stark consigned himself to their care.

An hour later, washed and shaved and dressed in a clean tunic, he was finishing the last of a solid meal when the man came again and said that Jerann required him in the council hall.

Freed of his shackles, Jerann was tall, erect and soldierly. He still had that look of fierce pride, but he was under no illusions.

"We are all fated men now," he said. "We can only go where our destiny leads us, and that may be to a place we would rather not see. Nevertheless, it is done. And march we shall."

He gave Stark a long, hard, measuring look. All the members of the Council were doing the same, and Stark knew what they were thinking. Why an off-worlder? Why does he bring with him this sudden stunning break from all history, all custom, all the laws under which we have endured? What has he really brought us—freedom and a new life, or death and utter destruction?

Stark had no answer for them. The prophecy said only that he would destroy the Lords Protector. It did not say what the result of that would be.

"Now, Eric John Stark, Earthman, tell us how you came to Skaith, how you came to Irnan, and why."

Stark knew perfectly well that Jerann had already heard the story, but he told it again, carefully and in detail. He told them about Ashton, and about Pax, and about how the matter of emigration stood with the Ministry of Planetary Affairs.

"I see," said Jerann. "Then it seems that we must believe in Dark Men and prophecies, and go our way in blind hope."

"What about the other city-states?" asked Stark. "They must be in much the same case as Irnan. Will they rise to help you?"

"I don't know. We'll do what we can to persuade them, naturally. But I think most of them will wait and see."

"Wait and see what?"

"If the prophecy is true." Jerann turned to an aide. "Have the Izvandian brought to me." The man hurried away, and Jerann said to Stark, "We must all know that, as soon as possible."

There was a wait, an awkwardness, a vacuum of uneasy silence within the encompassing sounds of triumph from outside in the streets. The members of the Council were tired and showing strain. The enormity of the commitment that Irnan had made this day must be weighing on them very heavily.

A knot of people came in, clustered round one tall lint-haired warrior. Stark noticed the gold ornaments on his harness, the torque and armbands. A chief, probably captain of the mercenaries. He was marched up the hall to where the Council sat, and he stood facing Jerann without emotion.

Jerann said coldly, "Greetings, Kazimni."

The Izvandian said, "I see you, Jerann."

Jerann took up a small heavy sack from the table. "This is the gold which is owed to you."

"To my dead as well? There are families."

"To your dead as well." He weighed the sack in his hand. "And there is in addition half as much again."

"If you wish to bribe us to leave Irnan," said Kazimni contemptuously, "keep your gold. We have no further business here."

Jerann shook his head. "No bribe. Payment for services."

Kazimni cocked one pale insolent eyebrow. "Oh?"

"Some of our people are going into the Barrens. A small party. We want you to escort them as far as Izvand."

Kazimni did not bother to ask why a party of Irnanese were going into the Barrens. It was no concern of his.

"Very well," he said. "Give us leave to bury our dead and make ready for the journey. We'll go when Old Sun rises." And he added, "With our arms."

"With your arms," said Jerann. He gave Kazimni the gold and said to the Irnanese escort, "You heard. Let them bury their dead, and give them what they need of supplies."

"Better to give them the sword," muttered one of the Irnanese. But they took Kazimni away obediently enough.

Stark asked, "Why Izvand?"

"Because it is that much closer to the Citadel. And for that distance you will have the protection of an escort. From there you must make your own arrangements, and I warn you—do not underestimate the dangers."

"Where exactly is this Citadel? Where is Worldheart?"

"I can tell you where tradition puts them. The fact you will learn for yourself."

"The Wandsmen know."

"Yes. But none are left alive in Irnan to tell us."

So that was no help. "Where is Gerrith?"

"She returned to her own place."

"Is that safe? The countryside must be full of wandering Farers."

"She's well guarded," Jerann said. "You'll see her in the morning. Go now and rest. It's a long road you've come, and a longer one you'll be taking tomorrow."

All night, in the intervals of sleep, Stark could hear the restless voices of the city, where preparations were being made for war. The revolt was well begun. But it was only a beginning, and it seemed a large order to turn an entire planet upside down just so two men, and off-worlders at that, could escape from it. Still, that order had been handed to him with no solicitation on his part, and at this moment he could see no other way out.

Well, he thought, that was for the future, and it was Gerrith's job to look ahead, not his. He would leave it to her. He slept, and in the dark morning he rose and dressed and was waiting patiently when a man came to waken him.

Jerann was below in the council hall. Stark thought that he had been there all night. Halk was there too, and Breca and two others of Yarrod's party.

"I am sorry," the old man said, "that Irnan cannot spare you the men you ought to have. We need them here."

Halk said, "We'll have to rely on being quick and hard to see. But with the Dark Man to lead us, how can we fail?"

Stark, who would just as soon have gone alone, said nothing. Food was brought, and strong bitter beer. When they had eaten, Jerann rose and said,

"It is time. I'll ride with you as far as the wise woman's grotto."

The square was eerily quiet in the chill first light of dawn. Some of the bodies had been taken away. Others were piled stiffly together, awaiting the carts. The tree-bark women had gone. Sentries manned the wall and the guard-towers by the gate.

The Izvandians, about sixty of them, were already mounted, men and animals alike blowing steam in the cold air. Beasts had been brought for Stark and his party. They mounted and fell in behind the troop, where Kazimni rode by and gave them a curt greeting.

Old Sun came up. The gates creaked open. The cavalcade moved out.

The road, so crowded and noisy the day before, was deserted except for the occasional dead. Some of the Farers had not run fast enough. Morning mist rose thick and white from the fields, and there was a fresh clean smell of growing things. Stark breathed deeply.

He became aware that Jerann was watching him. "You're glad to leave the city. You don't like being within walls."

Stark laughed. "I didn't realize it was so apparent."

"I am not acquainted with Earthmen," said Jerann courteously. "Are they all like you?"

"They find me quite as strange as you do." His eyes held a cruel gleam of amusement. "Perhaps even stranger."

The old man nodded. "Gerrith said—"

"A wolf's-head, a landless man, a man without a tribe. I was raised by animals, Jerann. That is why I seem like one." He lifted his head, looking northward. "Earthmen killed them all. They would have killed me too, except for Ashton."

Jerann glanced at Stark's face and shivered slightly. He did not speak again until, at the upper end of the valley, they reached the wise woman's grotto.

10

Only Stark and Jerann turned aside. The cavalcade went on, moving at a steady walking pace that covered a surprising amount of ground without tiring the animals. Stark could catch up with them easily. He slid off the soft, wooly-haired hide of the saddle-pad and followed Jerann up a steep path that wound through a dark overhanging wood. Finally they came to a hillside where the naked rock jutted out, forming rough pillars on either side of a cave. A party of men on guard there rose from around their fire and spoke to Jerann. The wise woman was within, and safe.

Inside the cave mouth was an antechamber, where Stark supposed that folk must wait to hear the oracle. At the far end were heavy curtains of some purple stuff that looked as if it had done duty for many Gerriths, and there were solemn designs embroidered in black. All in all, not a cheerful room. And cold, with the dusty tomb-smell of places shut away forever from the sun.

A tall old woman parted the curtains and signed to them to enter. She wore a long gray gown and her face was all bony sternness. She looked at Stark as though she would tear him with her sharp gaze, rip away his flesh and see what was beneath it.

"My old mistress died because of you," she said. "I hope it was not for nothing."

"So do I," said Stark, and stepped past her into the inner room.

This was somewhat better. There were rugs and hangings to soften the stone, pierced lamps for light and a brazier for warmth. But it was still a cave, and Gerrith looked out of place in it with her youth and her golden coloring. She was made for sunlight.

She sat in a massive chair behind a massive table. A wide, shallow bowl of silver stood on the table, filled with clear water.

"The Water of Vision," she said, and shook her head. "It has given me nothing." There were shadows around her eyes and her face was drawn, as though she had sat there all night. "I never had my mother's gift. I never wanted it, though she told me it would come in its own time, whether I wanted it or not. My own gift is small and not to be ordered. It's worse than having none at all. Always before I was able to use the Crown, and I think something of my mother and all the other Gerriths down through the centuries—the name is a tradition with us, Stark—lived on in it and could speak through it. Now there is no Crown and, as Mordach said, no wise woman in Irnan."

Stark took from his girdle an object wrapped in a bit of cloth and handed it to her.

"This is all that was left."

She opened the wrapping. The little yellow skull grinned up at her. Her face changed. "It is enough," she said. She leaned over the bowl, holding the skull between her hands. The water rippled as though in a sudden wind, and then was still.

Stark and Jerann waited, silent. And it seemed to Stark that the clear water turned red and thick and that shapes moved in it, shapes that brought the hackles prickling up at the back of his neck and stirred a small sound in his throat.

Gerrith looked up at him, startled. "You saw?"

"Not really." The water was clear again. "What were they?"

"Whatever they are, they stand between you and the Citadel." She stood up. "And I must go with you."

Jerann said, "But Lady! You can't leave Irnan now . . ."

"My work in Irnan is finished. I told you that. Now the Water of Vision has shown me where my path lies."

"Has it shown you what the end of that path will be?"

"No. You must find your own strength and your own faith, Jerann." She smiled at him, with genuine affection. "You've never lacked for either. Go back to your people, and if you have time now and again, pray for us."

She turned suddenly and laughed at Stark. "Not so downcast, Dark Man. I'll not burden you with bowls and braziers and tripods. Only this." She placed the little skull in a pouch at her girdle. "And I can ride and shoot as well as any." She called to the old woman and disappeared through the hangings into some inner chamber.

Jerann looked at Stark. There did not seem to be anything to say. They nodded to each other and Jerann left. Stark waited, scowling at the placid water in the silver bowl and cursing wise women. Whatever it was he had glimpsed there, he would as soon not have seen until the time came.

In a short time Gerrith returned, wearing tunic and riding cloak. She and Stark went together out of the cave and down the steep path, and the old woman stood in the cave entrance and watched them with eyes like cold steel daggers. Stark was glad when the trees hid them from her sight. At the foot of the path a gnarled old man had brought Gerrith's mount, with a sack of provisions tied to the saddle pad. She thanked him and bade him goodbye, and they rode away.

They came up with the party around noon, when Old Sun threw rusty shadows under the bellies of the beasts. Halk shrugged when he saw Gerrith.

"We shall have all the bogles on our side now," he said, and his mouth twisted in what might pass for a smile. "At least we see that the wise woman has enough faith in her mother's prophecy to put herself in danger."

They moved steadily toward the Barrens, following the Lamp of the North.

At first the road ran between mountains. There were peel-towers on the ridges, falling down, and ruins of fortified villages stuck to the cliffs like wasps' nests. But the mountains were still inhabited. For three days a band of very shaggy people followed them, going along their own secret trails parallel to the road. They carried crude weapons and ran with a curious loping stride, bent forward from the waist.

"One of the Wild Bands," Gerrith said. "They have no law at all except that of blind survival. They even come as far as Irnan sometimes. The Wandsmen hate them because they kill Wandsmen and Farers as readily as they kill us."

The Izvandian escort was too strong to be attacked, and there were no stragglers. At night, beyond the meager fires, Stark could hear stealthy rustlings, and several times the Izvandian sentries loosed arrows at things creeping toward the picket lines. They killed one of the intruders and Stark looked at the body in the light of morning. His nose wrinkled. "Why do they want to survive?" he wondered.

Halk said, "The vermin are leaving it. Stand back."

They left the heap of bones unburied on the stony ground.

The mountains dwindled away into hills covered with a dark, stunted scrub. Beyond them the land flattened out to the horizon, a treeless immensity of white and gray-green, a spongy mossiness flecked with a million icy ponds. The wind blew, sometimes hard, sometimes harder. Old Sun grew more feeble by the day. The Irnanese were stoical, riding the cold hours uncomplaining, wrapped in frosty cloaks. The Izvandians were comfortable and gay. This was their own, their native land.

Stark rode often beside Kazimni.

"In the days when Old Sun was young," Kazimni would say, and spin out one of the thousand or so legends he seemed to have at his fingertips, all of warmth and richness and the fatness of the land. The men of those days had been giants, the women beautiful and willing beyond belief. Warriors had magic weapons that killed from afar; fishermen had magic boats that sailed the skies. "Now it is as you see it," he would finish. "But we survive. We are strong. We are happy."

"Good," said Stark on one occasion. "I congratulate you. And where is this place they call Worldheart?"

Kazimni shrugged. "North."

"That's all you know?"

"Yes. If it exists at all."

"You sound as if you don't believe in the Lords Protector."

Kazimni's wolf-face expressed aristocratic scorn. "We do not require them. It makes little difference whether we believe in them or not."

"Yet you sell your swords to the Wandsmen."

"Gold is gold, and the Wandsmen have more of it than most. We do not have to like them, or follow their religion. We're free men. All the People of the Barrens are free. Not all of us are good. Some do business with the Wandsmen, some do not. Some trade with the city-states; some trade with each other; some do not trade at all but live by rapine. Some are mad. Quite mad. But free. There are no Farers here, and we can defend ourselves. The Wandsmen have found poor pickings among us. They let us alone."

"I see," said Stark, and rode for a time in silence. "Something lives in that place by Worldheart," he said at last. "Something not human, and yet not quite animal."

Kazimni gave a sidelong glance out of his tilted yellow eyes. "How do you know that?"

"Perhaps the wind whispered it to me."

"Or perhaps the wise woman."

"What are they, Kazimni?"

"We're great talkers here in the Barrens. Great tellers of tales. We fill the winter nights with talk. When our throats go dry with it we wet them with more khamm and talk again."

"What are they?"

"The Harsenyi nomads bring us tales, and so do the darkland traders. Sometimes they winter with us at Izvand, and those are good winters." He paused. "I have heard stories of Northhounds."

Stark repeated the name. "Northhounds." It had a solemn ring to it.

"I can't tell you if the stories are true. Men lie without meaning to. They talk as if they had been part of a thing that happened to someone they never knew and only heard of by sixth remove. Northhounds are a sort of demon to the Harsenyi, and to some of the traders. Monsters that appear out of the snow-mist and do terrible things. It is said that the Lords Protector created them long ago, to guard their Citadel. It is said that they still guard it, and woe take any wanderer who stumbles into their domain."

Hairs prickled briefly at the back of Stark's neck, just at the memory of those shapes he had seen in the Water of Vision. "I think you can believe in Northhounds, Kazimni." He changed the subject. "Is that why your people are content with life in the Barrens—because they are free?"

"Is it not enough?" Kazimni jerked his chin contemptuously toward the Irnanese. "If we lived soft, as they do, we too would be slaves, as they are."

Stark could understand that. "You must have known what brought on the trouble at Irnan."

"Yes. Good trouble. As soon as we've rested and seen our wives, we'll be back on the Border. There'll be need of fighting men."

"No doubt. But how would your people feel about emigrating?"

"To another world?" Kazimni shook his head. "The land shapes us. We are what we are because of it. If we were in another place, we would be another people. No.

Old Sun will last us yet a while. And life in the Barrens is not so bad. You will see that when we come to Izvand."

The road looped and wound among the frozen ponds. There were other travelers on it, though not as many as in the Fertile Belt. They were of a different breed, darker and grimmer than the flotsam of the southern roads. There was a good deal of trade back and forth across the border; drovers with herds for the markets of Izvand and Komrey, merchants with wagon-loads of grain and wool, strings of pack-animals carrying manufactured goods from the southern workshops, long lines of great creaking wains hauling timber from some far place in the mountains. Coming the other way were caravans bringing furs and salt and dried fish. All traveled in groups, well armed, each lot keeping to itself. There were inns and rest-houses along the way but Kazimni avoided them, preferring to camp in the open. "Thieves and robbers," he said of the inn-keepers. And of the accommodations, "They stink."

The Izvandians moved rapidly, passing everything else on the road. And yet sometimes Stark felt as though that movement was only an illusion and they were trapped forever in the unchanging landscape.

Gerrith felt his impatience. "I share it," she told him. "For you, one man. For me, a people. Yet things must go at their own pace."

"Does your gift tell you that?"

She smiled at him. It was night, with the Three Ladies shining through gaps in scudding cloud-wrack. They were in an unfamiliar quarter of the sky now, but still beautiful. Old friends. Stark had grown quite fond of them. Nearer at hand, the light of a little fire flared and flickered across Gerrith's face.

"Something tells me. Everything is in train now, and the end has already been written. We have only to meet it."

Stark grunted, unconvinced. The beasts, huddled together with their tails to the wind, munched at heaps of moss piled up for them. The Izvandians laughed and chattered around their fires. The Irnanese were wrapped bundles, suffering in silence.

Gerrith said, "Why do you love this man Ashton so deeply?"

"But you know that. He saved my life."

"And so you cross the stars to risk losing it on a world you never heard of before? To go through all this when you know that he may already be dead? It's not enough, Stark. Will you tell me?"

"Tell you what?"

"Who you are. What you are. A lesser gift even than mine could sense that you're different. Inside, I mean. There's a stillness, something I can't touch. Tell me about you and Ashton."

So he told her, of his childhood on a cruel planet far too close to its sun, where the heat killed by day and the frost by night, where the sky thundered and the rocks split, where the ground shook and the mountains fell down.

"I was born there. We were part of a mining colony. A quake and a great fall of rock killed everyone but me. I'd have died too, but the People took me in. They were the aborigines. They weren't human, not quite. They still had their hairy pelts, and they didn't talk much, a few clicks and grunts, cries for hunting and warning and calling-together. They shared all they had with me."

Heat and cold and hunger. Those were the most of it. But their hairy bodies warmed his small nakedness in the bitter night, and their hard hands fed him. They taught him love, and patience, how to hunt the great rock-lizard, how to suffer, how to survive. He remembered their faces, wrinkled, snouted, toothed. Beautiful faces to him, beautiful and wise with the wisdom of first beginnings. His people. Always his people, his only people. And yet they had named him Man-Without-a-Tribe.

"More Earthmen came, in time," Stark said. "They needed the food and water the People were using, so they killed them. They were only animals. Me they put in a cage and kept for a curiosity. They poked sticks between the bars to make me snap and snarl at them. They were going to kill me too, when the novelty wore off. Then Ashton came."

Ashton the administrator, armed with the lightnings of authority. Stark smiled wryly.

"To me he was just another flat-faced enemy, something to be hated and killed. I'd lost all my human origins, of course, and the humans I'd met had given me little cause to love them. Ashton took me, all the same. I couldn't have been a very pleasant charge, but he had the patience of mountains. He tamed me. He taught me house manners, and how to speak in words, and most of all he taught me that while there are bad men, there are also good ones. Yes, he did give me much more than just my life."

"I understand now, " Gerrith said, and he thought she did, truly, as well as anyone could. She stirred the fire and sighed. "I'm sorry I can't tell you whether your friend is still alive."

"We'll know that soon enough," Stark said, and lay down on the cold ground and slept.

And dreamed.

He was following Old One up a cliff, angry because his feet did not have long clever toes, fiercely determined to make up for his deformity by climbing twice as hard and twice as high. The sun burned terribly on his naked back. The rock scorched him. Black peaks pierced the sky on all sides.

Old One slid without sound into a crevice, making the imperative sign. The boy N'Chaka crept in beside him. Old One pointed with his throwing-stick. High above them on a ledge, its huge jaws open in sensuous languor, a rock-lizard slept half-lidded in the sun.

With infinite care, moving one muscle at a time, his belly tight with emptiness and hope, the boy began again to follow Old One up the cliff—

He did not like the dream. It saddened him even in sleep, so that he started awake in order to escape it. He sat a long time by the dying fire, listening to the lonely sounds of the night. When he slept again it was without memories.

Next day, in the afternoon, they saw the roofs of a stockaded town by the shore of a frozen sea. With pride and affection, Kazimni said,

"There is Izvand."

11

It was a sturdy town, solidly built of timber brought from the mountains, with steep roofs to shed the snow. Izvand was the trade center for this part of the Inner Barrens, so that there was a constant coming and going of wagons and pack trains. Traffic churned the narrow streets by day, and at night the mud froze into ankle-breaking chaos. In the summer, Kazimni said, fishing was the business of many Izvandians, and as soon as the ice went out of the harbor the high-prowed boats would be hauled from their winter sheds.

"Not a bad life," he said. "Not bad at all. Plenty of food and fighting. Why don't you stay with us, Stark?"

Stark shook his head, and Kazimni shrugged. "Very well. This is the season for the darkland traders to start moving north. I'll see if I can arrange something. Meantime, I know a good inn."

The inn had a creaking sign, much weathered, depicting some large and improbable fish with horns. There were stabling and fodder for the beasts, and rooms for the people. These were small and cold, sleeping four apiece in two close-beds, and they had lacked soap and water for a long time. The common-room steamed with warmth and sweat and the not-unappetizing odor of fish soup. It was good to be warm again, to eat hot food and drink khamm, which was like sweet white lightning. Stark enjoyed these simple pleasures without guilt.

When he saw that the others were all finished he stood up, and Halk said, "Where are you going?"

"I have a mind to see the town."

"Don't you think we had better be planning what

we're going to do next?" He had drunk quite a bit of khamm.

"A little more information might help us decide," said Stark mildly. "In any case, we'll need warmer clothing and more provisions."

Without noticeable enthusiasm, the Irnanese rose and fetched their cloaks and followed him into the chilly street.

Halk. Breca, who was Halk's shield-mate. Gerrith. Atril and Wake, the brothers, two of Yarrod's picked men. Stark could not have asked for better. Yet they six were a small handful against the North. Not for the first time Stark considered slipping away from them to finish his journey alone and unencumbered.

He was surprised to hear Gerrith say softly, "No. Me at least you must have with you. Perhaps the others as well, I don't know. But if you go alone, you will fail."

"Your gift?" asked Stark, and she nodded.

"My gift. On that score it is quite clear."

The market was roofed against snow. Doors at the entrances shut out most of the cold wind. Smoky lamps and braziers burned. Merchants sat amid their wares, and Stark noticed that few of them were of Izvand. The pale-haired warriors apparently scorned such occupation.

The market was busy. The party from Irnan wandered with the crowd, buying furs and boots and sacks of the sweet, fatty journey-cake they make in Izvand against the cold. After a while Stark found what he was looking for, the street of the chart-makers.

It was a small street, lined with alcoves where men sat hunched over their drawing tables, surrounded on three sides by honeycomb shelves stuffed with rolls of parchment. Stark went from shop to shop, emerging at last with an armload of maps.

They went back to the inn. Stark found a relatively quiet table in a corner of the common-room and spread out his purchases.

The maps were for the use of traders, and in the essentials they agreed well enough. The roads, with inns and shelter-houses marked. Modern towns like Izvand, pegs to hold the roads together where they crossed. Vestiges, here and there, of older roads leading to older cities, and most of these marked ominously with death's heads. On other matters they were vaguer. Several of them showed Worldheart, hedged about with many warnings, but each one in a different place. Others did not show it at all, merely indicating a huge area of nothing with the comforting legend *Demons.*

"Somewhere in here," said Stark, setting his hand over the blank area. "If we keep going north, sooner or later we'll find someone who knows."

"So the maps don't help much," said Halk.

"You haven't looked closely," Gerrith said. "They all show one thing, and that is that we must travel by the road as far as we can." Her fingers flicked across the wrinkled parchment. "Here we are blocked by the sea, and here by a mountain wall. Here again, where the land is low, are lakes and bogs."

"All frozen now," Halk said.

"And impassable even so. The beasts would be dead or crippled and we would be starving before a week's end."

"Besides," said Wake, who always spoke for the brothers, "there is the matter of time. Irnan may already be under attack. Even if we could make it the other way, it would take too long."

Halk looked around the table. "You're all agreed?" They were. Halk tossed back another glass of khamm. "Very well. Let us go by the road, and go fast."

"That is another point," Stark said. "Whether to travel alone, or go with some trader. A trader's company would be safer . . ."

"If you could trust the trader."

". . . but we would be held to the wagon pace."

"We didn't make this journey to be safe," said Halk.

"For once, I agree with you," Stark said. "By the road, then, and alone." The others voiced assent. Stark bent over the maps again. "I'd give much to know where the Wandsmen's road runs."

"Not on these maps," said Gerrith. "They must go up from Skeg to the east, across the desert. There would be post-houses and wells, everything to get them quickly on their way."

"And safeguards, doubtless, to make sure that no one can follow them." Stark began rolling up the parchments. "We'll leave at the fourth hour. Best get some sleep."

"Not yet a few moments," said Breca, and nodded toward the inn door.

Kazimni had just entered, in company with a lean brown man in a furred cloak who moved with the agile, hungry, questing gait of a wolverine. Kazimni saw them, and the two came toward their table.

"I'll talk," said Stark quietly. "No comment, no matter what I say."

Kazimni hailed them with great cheer. "Greetings, friends! Here is one you will be glad to meet." He introduced his companion. "Amnir of Komrey." The man in the furred cloak bowed. His eyes, gleaming like brown beryls, darted from one face to another. His mouth smiled. "Amnir trades far into the darklands. He thinks he can be of help to you."

Stark invited the men to sit and introduced his party. The merchant ordered a round of khamm for all.

"Kazimni tells me that you have an errand northward," he said, when the glasses had arrived and the ceremonial first sip was taken. "What I think of the wisdom of that errand is neither here nor there." He glanced at the heap of parchments on the table. "I see you have bought maps."

"Yes."

"You were, perhaps, thinking of going on alone?"

"Hazardous, we know," said Stark. "Nevertheless, our errand is urgent."

"Better to make haste slowly than not at all," said Amnir sententiously. "There are wicked men in the Barrens. You can't know how wicked. Six of you—and all stout fighters, I'm sure—would be as nothing against those you will meet along the road."

"What would they want with us?" Stark asked. "We have nothing worth the stealing."

"You have yourselves," said Amnir. "Your bodies. Your strength." He bowed to the ladies. "Your beauty. Men and women are sold in the Barrens, for many purposes."

Halk said, "I think anyone who tried that would find us a poor bargain."

"No doubt. But why take the risk? If you're captured, or killed resisting capture, where is your errand then?" He leaned forward over the table. Sincerity shone within him. "I trade farther into the darklands than anyone because I am able to face the dangers there not only with courage, which many others have as well, but with prudence, which many others seem to lack. I travel with fifty well-armed men. Why not share that safety?"

Stark frowned, as though pondering. Halk seemed on the point of saying something, and Breca gave him a warning glare.

"All he says is true," Kazimni said. "By Old Sun, I swear it."

"The time, though." Stark shook his head. "Alone, we can move much faster."

"For a while," Amnir agreed. "And then—" He made a chopping gesture with the edge of his hand against his neck. "Besides, I'm no laggard, I can't afford to be. You'd not be losing much."

"When do you leave?"

"In the morning, before first light."

Again Stark seemed to ponder. "What price would you want?"

"No price. You'd find your own food and mounts, of course, and if we should be attacked you'd be expected to fight. That's all."

"What could be fairer?" asked Kazimni. "And look, if the pace proves to be too slow, you can always leave the wagons. Is that not so, Amnir?"

Amnir laughed. "I'd not be the one to stop them."

Stark looked across at Gerrith. "What does the wise woman say?"

"That we should do what the Dark Man thinks best."

"Well," said Stark, "if it's true that we can go our own way if we choose to later on—"

"Of course. Of course!"

"Then I think we ought to go with Amnir in the morning."

They struck hands on it. They drank more khamm. They arranged final details, and the two men left. Stark gathered his maps and led his party upstairs. They crowded into one of the small rooms.

"Now what does the wise woman say?" asked Stark.

"That Amnir of Komrey means us no good."

"It needs no wise woman to see that," said Halk. "The man smells of treachery. Yet the Dark Man has agreed to go with him."

"The Dark Man is not above telling lies when he thinks they're called for." Stark looked round at them. "We'll not wait for the fourth hour. As soon as the inn is quiet, we go. You can do your sleeping in the saddle."

In the star-blazing midnight, they rode out of Izvand. The cold ribbon of road stretched north toward the darklands, and they had it all to themselves. They made the most of it. Halk seemed to be consumed with a passion for haste, and Stark was in no mood to dispute him. He, too, wanted to leave Amnir as far behind as possible.

The land had begun its long slope upward to the ice-locked ranges of the north, and from the higher places Stark could keep a watchful eye on the backtrail. He could also sniff the wind and listen to the silence and feel the vast secret land that encircled him.

It was not a good land. The primitive in him sensed evil there like a sickness. It wanted to turn tail and go shivering and howling back to the smoky warmth of Izvand and the safety of walls. The reasoning man in him agreed, but kept moving forward nevertheless.

Clouds hid the Three Ladies. Snow began falling. Stark disliked the inability to see clearly; anything might come upon them out of those pale drifting clouds. The party rode more slowly, keeping close together.

They came upon an inn, crouched over a crossroads. It had a tall roof like a wizard's hat, and one slitted yellow eye. Stark considered stopping there and instantly decided against it. By common consent they left the road and made a wide circle round the inn, walking the beasts carefully so as to make no sound.

Daylight was slow in coming, and when Old Sun did show himself at last it was only as a smear of ginger-colored light behind a blur of snowflakes.

It was in that strange brassy glow that they came to the bridge.

12

The bridge, the rocky gorge it spanned, and the village that existed solely to administer to and extort for the bridge, were clearly marked on all the maps. There was apparently no way around that did not take at least a week, even without snow, and the toll seemed reasonable. Stark loosened his sword in its scabbard and dug some coins from the leather bag that hung about his neck underneath the bulky furs. The Irnanese checked their own weapons.

In close order, they trotted themselves and their pack animals toward the toll-house, a squat blocky structure commanding the southern end of the bridge. An identical structure was at the northern end. Each building contained a winch that raised or lowered a portion of the bridge floor, so that no one could force his way through without paying. You might take one toll-house but never both, and a part of the bridge would always be unreachably open. The drop below it was unpleasant, several hundred feet down past jagged boulders rimed with snow and frozen spray to a vicious little river that drained some glacier slope higher up. The village was built on the southern side, against the face of a low cliff, strongly fortified. Stark guessed that the convenience of the bridge outweighed the nuisance factor, and so generations of merchants had let it survive.

Three men came out of the building. Short, broad and ugly troll-like men, with many furs and too-wide smiles. They smelled.

"How much?" asked Stark.

"For how large a party?" Small eyes probed the

77

snowfall behind them. "How many beasts? How many wagons? The bridge floor suffers. Lumber is costly. Planks must be replaced. This is heavy labor, and our children starve to pay for the wood."

"No wagons," said Stark. "A dozen beasts. What you see."

Three faces stared in disbelief. "Six persons, traveling alone?"

Again Stark asked, "How much?"

"Ah. Um," said the chief of the three men, suddenly animated. "For so small a party, a small price." He named it. Stark leaned down and counted the coins into his grimy palm. It seemed, indeed, too small a price. The men departed chattering into the toll-house. They had some way of signaling to the other side of the gorge, and presently both sections of the bridge went creaking down into position.

Stark and the Irnanese rode onto the bridge.

The signaling was very effective, because before they could reach the other side the northern section of the bridge shot upward again, leaving a large cold gap to death.

"All right, then," said Stark wearily, "we fight."

They turned, with the intention of bolting back off the bridge, but a flight of arrows came from slits in the toll-house wall and thumped into the planking in front of them.

"Stand where you are!" a voice shouted. "Lay down your weapons."

A whole band of trolls, furred and armed, came waddling at speed from the village. Stark looked at the nasty little slits in the wall, where more arrow-tips were visible. "I think we're fairly caught," he said. "Shall we live a little longer, or die now?"

"Live," said Gerrith.

They laid their weapons down and stood where they were. The villagers swarmed onto the bridge and took them, dragging them out of the saddle, pushing, pummelling, laughing. The beasts were led off and tethered to a rack by the toll-house. The bridge-keeper and his friends came out.

"Six persons traveling alone!" said the bridge-keeper, and lifted his hands to the brassy glow in the south. "Old Sun, we thank you for sending us fools." He turned and pawed at Stark's garments, searching for the purse.

Stark resisted a strong impulse to tear the man's throat out with his teeth. Halk, who was being similarly handled, got his hands free and fought. He was immediately clubbed down.

"Don't damage him," said the bridge-keeper. "All that muscle is worth its weight in iron." He found the purse and slashed the thong that held it, then prodded at Stark's chest with his dirty fingers. "This one, too—all strong big men, the four of them. Good, good! And the women—" He cackled, skipping on his thick feet. "Maybe we'll keep them here for a while, eh? Until we're tired, eh? Look at them, lads, and their damned long legs—"

Gerrith said, "I was wrong. It would have been better to die."

And Stark answered, "Listen."

It was difficult to hear anything over the chattering of the villagers, and her ears were not as keen as his. But as the sounds swept nearer she heard, and then everybody heard; the rush of hoofbeats, the jingle of harness, the clash of arms. Riders appeared out of the falling snow. They came in strength, they came like the wind, their lances were sharp, and Amnir of Komrey was at their head.

The villagers turned and ran.

"Oh, no," said Amnir, and the riders herded them back, jabbing them painfully so that they leapt and screamed. The bridge-keeper stood stock still with Stark's purse in his hand.

"You have broken the covenant," Amnir said. "The

covenant by which we let you live, which is that once a man has paid fair toll for his passage across your bridge, he shall pass without let or hindrance."

"But," said the bridge-keeper, "six persons alone— such fools are doomed in any case. Could I spurn the gift of Old Sun? It is seldom enough that he sends us one."

Amnir's hard eyes looked down upon him. Amnir's lance-tip pricked his throat. "That which is in your hand. Does it belong to you?"

The man shook his head. He let the purse drop with a small heavy clink at his feet.

"What shall I do," asked Amnir, "with you and your people?"

"Lord," said the bridge-keeper, "I'm a poor man. My back is broken from the labor of the bridge. My children starve."

"Your children," said Amnir, "are as fat as hogs and twice as dirty. As for your back, it's fit enough for thieving."

The bridge-keeper spread his hands. "Lord, I'm greedy. I saw a chance for profit and I took it. Any man would do the same."

"Well," said Amnir, "and that is true. Or nearly so."

"You can slay us, of course," said the bridge-keeper, "but then who will do our work? Think of the time it will cost you. Think of the wealth you will lose." He shuddered. "Think of the Gray Feeders. Perhaps even you, lord, might make your end upon their hooks."

"It does not become you, at this time, to threaten me," said Amnir, and thrust a little harder with his lance.

The bridge-keeper sighed. Two large tears formed and rolled down his cheeks. "Lord, I am in your hands," he said, and wilted inside his furs.

"Hm," said Amnir. "If I spare you, will you keep the covenant?"

"Forever!"

"Which means until the next time you think you can safely break it." He turned in the saddle and shouted. "Back to your sties, filthy ones! Go!"

The villagers fled. The bridge-keeper wept and tried to embrace Amnir's off-side knee.

"Free passage, lord! For you, no toll."

"I'm touched," said Amnir. "And pray remove your dirty paws." The bridge-keeper scuttled, bowing himself backward, into the toll-house. Amnir dismounted and came to Stark and his party. Halk, bloodied and furious, had been helped to his feet.

"I warned you," said Amnir. "Did I not warn you?"

"You did." Stark looked past him at the riders, seeing how they had moved quietly to form a half-circle of lances that pinned the unarmed Irnanese against the end of the open bridge. "You must have ridden hard to overtake us."

"Very hard. You ought to have waited, Stark. You ought to have gone with my wagons. What was the matter? Didn't you trust me?"

Stark said, "No."

"You were wise," said Amnir, and smiled. He motioned to his men. "Take them."

13

The Three Ladies were remote, withdrawn, scarcely showing their faces. The Lamp of the North, like a burning emerald, dominated the sky. The short days of the darklands were little brighter than the nights. Old Sun's dull gleaming stained the sky rather than brightened it. The white snow turned the color of rust, and the vast plain, strewn with the wrecks of abandoned cities, tilted upward to a distant wall of mountains all dabbled in the same red-ochre. The line of great wagons creaked and crawled across this unreal landscape, sixteen of them with canvas tops booming in the wind. From long before sunrise until long after dark the wagons moved, and when they halted they made their own fort, with the beasts and the people inside.

Stark and the Irnanese rode their own mounts and were fed from the rations they had bought at Izvand. Amnir was delighted that their transportation was costing him nothing. Each mount was led by an armed rider. The captives had their fur-gloved hands bound and their fur-booted ankles tied together with a thong under the animal's belly. The bonds were arranged expertly to hold without impeding circulation, so that the extremities should not freeze.

Uncomfortable as this was, it was an improvement over the first days, when Amnir kept them close in the wagons, away from curious eyes. Other parties of armed merchants were on the roads, and Amnir had business at two or three centers where itinerant traders like the Harsenyi nomads brought their wares. These places were like blockhouses, with crude shelters around them where travelers might find some respite from snow and wind. Amnir stayed away from the shelters. He seemed to have no friends among the darkland traders. His men did not mingle with men of other wagon trains, but remained aloof and perpetually on guard.

At the last of the centers there was an altercation with some wild-looking people bringing in a string of little shaggy beasts loaded with bundles. These people called Amnir unpleasant names in a barbarous dialect. They threw stones and clots of ice. Amnir's men stood ready but no real attack developed and the wild ones withdrew once they had worked off their bad tempers.

Amnir was not disturbed. "I took a large portion of their trade away from them," he said. "It was necessary to kill some of them. Let them yabble at me, if it gives them pleasure."

After that they left the marked roads and went off into this enormous emptiness, where the wagons followed a dim and ancient track that was only apparent when it went through some cut or over a causeway that showed an engineering skill long lost on Skaith.

"An old road," said Amnir. "Once, when Old Sun was young, all this land was rich and there were great cities. This road served them. Folk didn't ride on beasts in those days, or drive clumsy wagons. They had machines, bright shining things as swift as the wind. Or if they wanted to they could take wing and rush through the sky like shooting stars. Now we plod, as you see, across the cold corpse of our world."

But a note of pride was in his voice when he said it. *We are men, we survive, we are not defeated.*

"For what purpose," asked Stark, "do we plod?"

Amnir had refused to tell them what he intended doing with them. It was obvious from the pleased speculative looks he gave them that he had large plans. Whatever they might be, Kazimni had certainly had a part in making them and would share in the profits. Stark bore Kazimni no ill-will for that. He had done his task honorably, getting the party safely to Izvand. Nothing had been said about getting them safely out again.

Knowing perfectly well what Stark wanted, Amnir smiled and evaded.

"Trade," he said. "Wealth. I told you that I trade farther into the darklands than others, and this is the way of it. Metal ingots kept appearing in the market-places of Komrey and Izvand, ingots unlike any I had seen before. Ingots of a superior quality, stamped with a hammer mark. My centers of greed are highly developed. They began to deliver certain juices which stimulate curiosity and the ability to scent profit. I traced these ingots back through a long and complicated chain of trade carried on by such as you saw back there with their bundles. Men died in that tracing, but I found the source."

He was riding, as he often did, beside Stark, whiling away the long cold hours with talk.

"These people of the ingots love me. They look upon me as their benefactor. Formerly they were at the mercy of many things: accident, loss, theft, stupidity, the haphazards of going through many hands. Now that I give them direct and honest trade, they have become so rich and fat that they no longer have to eat each other. Of course, because of this, their population is growing, and one day some of them will have to leave Thyra and find another city."

"Thyra," said Stark. "A city. One of those marked with a death's head?"

"Yes," said Amnir. He smiled.

"But they no longer have to eat each other."

"No," said Amnir, and smiled the wider. "Pray that we reach it, Earthman. There is worse between." And he added fiercely, "No great profit is made without risk."

Stark kept a watchful eye on the landscape. As they went farther on he was sure that he saw, in the rusty gloom, pale things slipping furtively behind hillocks and into ravines. They were distant. They were silent. Perhaps they were only shadows. In this light, vision became confused. In the moonless mornings and afternoons, one could be sure of nothing. Still, he watched.

In those moonless hours, Amnir would now and again stare up at the stars, as though for the first time in his life he was thinking of them as suns with families of planets, other worlds with other people and other ways. He seemed not entirely happy with the thought, and he blamed Stark for having brought it home to him.

"Skeg was a long way off. We had heard about the ships, and the strangers, but we thought little of it. We never quite believed. It was too large a thought, too strange. We had enough to think about without that. Eating. Drinking. Begetting children. I have six sons, did you know that? And daughters as well. I have wives. I have family matters. I have property. Many people depend upon me for their livelihood. I have matters of trade to consider, to judge and act upon. These things take up my days, my years, my life. They are quite sufficient.

"Like the Izvandians, we of Komrey are descended from folk who came originally from the high north, who did not wish to go farther south than was necessary to sustain our way of life. We remained in the Barrens by choice. We consider the people of the city-states, like the Irnanese, to be soft and corrupt." He glared at the stars as though he hated them. "One is born on a world. It may not be perfect, but it's the world one knows, the only world. One adjusts, one survives. Then suddenly it appears that there is no need to struggle because one has a choice of many worlds. It's confusing. It shakes the whole foundation of life. Why do we need it?"

"It isn't a question of whether or not you need it," said Stark. "It's there. You can use it or not, as you please."

"But it makes everything so pointless! Take the Thyrans. I've heard all their ballads, *The Long Wandering, The Destruction of the Red Hunters, The Coming of Strayer*—he's the folk-hero who is supposed to have taught them how to work metal, though I suspect there were many Strayers—*The Conquest of the Mountain,* and so on. The long dark years, the courage, the dying and the pain, and finally the triumph. And now we see that if they had only known it, they could have run away to a better world and avoided all that." Amnir shook his head. "I don't like it. I believe in a man staying by what he knows."

Stark refused to argue this. And then Amnir's curiosity would betray him and he would ask how it was on other worlds, how the people ate and dressed and traded and made love, and if they really were *people*. Stark took a wicked pleasure in answering, unstitching Amnir's self-assurance, opening up the wide heavens to show him a thousand places where Amnir-out-of-context would not exist.

Amnir had a way of setting his jaw. "I don't care. I am myself, I've fought my fight and made my place. I ask for nothing better."

Stark played the tempter. "But it makes you a little dissatisfied, doesn't it? You're a greedy man. Do you see the great ships coming and going between the suns, bearing cargoes you haven't got a name for, worth more money than your small horizon can hold? You could have a ship of your own, Amnir, just for the asking."

"If I set you free. If you succeed. If, if. The odds are too long. Besides—I am a greedy man, yes, but a wise greedy man. I know my small horizon. It fits me. The stars do not."

As a matter of policy, Amnir kept his captives apart. There was less likelihood of mischief, and he knew that the thought of escape was always in their minds. Stark could see the others, hooded and wrapped in furs like himself, riding their led beasts, but he had no chance to talk to them. He wondered what Gerrith would be thinking now about the prophecy.

Halk made one desperate, ill-considered attempt at

breaking away, and after that he was confined to one of the wagons. At night they were all put inside. Stark was bound to the wagon frame in such a way that he could not bring his hands together nor get at the tough thong with his teeth. Each time they bound him he tested the bonds to see if they had been careless. When he found they had not, he lay on the bales of goods that formed his bed and slept, with the iron patience of a wild thing. He had not forgotten Ashton. He had not forgotten anything. He was simply waiting. And every day brought him closer to where he wanted to go.

He asked Amnir about the Citadel.

Amnir said, "All of you have asked me the same question. I give you all the same answer. Ask the Thyrans."

He smiled. Stark was getting bored with his everlasting smiles.

"How long have you been trading this far north?"

"If I complete it, this will be my seventh journey."

"Do you feel there's a chance you may not complete it?"

"On Skaith," said Amnir, for once not smiling, "there is always that chance."

The ruins became more extensive. In places they were no more than shapeless hummocks of ice and snow. In others there were stumps of towers still standing, and great mazes of walls and pits. Several sorts of creatures laired in the hollow places. They seemed to live by hunting each other, and the more aggressive ones came howling and prowling around the wagons at night to put the beasts in an uproar.

Twice the wagons were attacked in force, and by day. It seemed that the squat ferocious shapes emerged from the ground itself, rushing forward in the rusty twilight, hurling themselves at anything that lived, all teeth and talons and wild harsh screamings. They impaled themselves on lances, spitted themselves on swords, and their fellows tore them to bits and devoured them while still they screamed. The armed men drove them off, but in each case not before some of the beasts had been pulled down in harness by swarming bodies and reduced to stripped bones in a matter of minutes. The creatures did not stop eating even long enough to die. The worst thing about it to Stark was that the overpowering stench of them was undeniably human.

As they passed these danger points in the ruins, the shadows that slipped and slid along the edges of vision disappeared, only to reappear farther on.

It was obvious that Amnir had been aware of them, too, and that he was worried.

"You know who they are?"

"They call themselves the People of the Towers. The Thyrans say they're great magicians. The Gray Maggots, they call them, and will have nothing to do with them. I've always paid them a generous tribute for passage through their city, and we've had no trouble. But they've never done this before, this spying and following. I don't understand it."

"How soon do we reach their city?"

"Tomorrow," said Amnir, and his hand tightened on his sword hilt.

In the dark morning-time, under the green star, they crossed a river on the ice, beside the piers of a vanished bridge. On the other side of the river a cluster of towers reared against the sky, jagged and broken in outline. They were perfectly silent, except for the wind. But they showed lights.

The road ran straight to the towers. Stark looked at them with immense distaste. Ice glazed them. Snow choked their crevices, frosted their shattered edges. It was somehow indecent that there should be lights within those walls.

Amnir rode along the line of wagons. "Close up there. Close up. Smartly now! Let them see your weapons. On your guard, watch my lance point, and keep moving."

The broken towers were grouped around an open circle, which had a huge lump of something in the middle that might once have been a monument to civic pride. Three figures stood beside the monument. They were gaunt. tuck-bellied, long-armed, slightly stooped. They wore tight-fitting garments of an indeterminate gray color, hoods covering narrow heads. Their faces were masked against the wind. The masks were worked in darker threads with what appeared to be symbols of rank. The three stood immobile, alone, and the ragged doorways of the buildings gaped darkly on either hand.

Stark's nostrils twitched. A smell of living came to him from those doorways—a dry subtle taint of close-packed bodies, of smoke and penned animals, of dung and wool and unnameable foods. He was riding in his usual place beside the third wagon in line. Gerrith was behind him, beside the fourth; the other captives strung out behind her, except for Halk, who was still confined. Stark tugged nervously at his bonds, and the armed man who led his beast thumped him with his lance butt and bade him be still.

The noise of the wagons rolled against the silence. Amnir rode aside, toward the three gray figures. Men came after him bearing sacks and bales and rolls of cloth.

Amnir halted and raised his hand. The hand held a lance, point upward.

"May Old Sun give you light and warmth, Hargoth."

"There is neither here," said the foremost figure. Only his eyes and his mouth showed. The eyes were pale and unreadable. Above them, on the forehead of the mask, was the winged-disc sun-symbol which Stark had found to be almost universal. On the sides of the mask, covering the cheeks, were stylized grain patterns. Stark supposed the man was both chief and high priest. It was strange to find a Corn King here, where no corn had grown for centuries. The man's mouth had thin lips and very sharp teeth. His voice was high and reedy but it had a carrying quality, a note of authority.

"Here there are only my lord Darkness, and his lady Cold, and their daughter Hunger."

"I have brought you gifts," said Amnir.

And the Corn King said, "This time, you have brought us more."

The wind blew his words away. But Amnir's lance point dipped and a movement began along the line of wagons, a bristling of weapons. The man leading Stark's beast shortened up on the rein.

In a curiously flat tone Amnir said, "I don't take your meaning."

"Why should you?" said the Corn King. "You have not the Sight. But I have seen. I have seen it in the Winter Dreaming. I have seen it in the entrails of the Spring Child that we give each year to Old Sun. I have seen it in the stars. Our guide has come, the Promised One who will lead us into the far heavens, into warmth and light. He is with you now." A long slender arm shot out and pointed straight at Stark. "Give him to us."

"I do not understand you," Amnir said. "I have only captives from the south, to be sold as slaves to the Thyrans."

The lance point dipped lower. The pace of the wagons quickened.

"You lie," said the Corn King. "You will sell them to the Citadel. Word has come from the high north, both truth and lies, and we know the difference. There are strangers on Skaith, and the star-roads are open. We have waited through the long night, and now it is morning."

As though in answer, the first sullen glimmer of dawn stained the eastern sky.

"Give us our guide now. Only death waits for him in the high north."

Stark shouted, "What word have you of strangers?"

The armed man clouted him hard across the head

with the lance butt. Amnir voiced a shrill cry, reining his beast around, and the wagons began to move, faster and faster, the teams slipping and scrabbling on the frosty ground.

14

Bound so that he could neither fight nor fall, half unconscious from the blow, Stark saw the encircling walls and
dark doorways rush past him in a ringing haze. He
wanted the people inside those doorways to come out
and attack, to set him free, but they did not. And the
Corn King with his attendants remained motionless beside the monument. In a few moments the whole clatter-
ing, jouncing caravan of wagons and armed men was
clear of the circle and racing along between lesser ruins,
lightless and deserted. By the time Old Sun had dragged
himself above the horizon they were in open country,
and unpursued.

Amnir halted the train to rest the beasts and restore
order along the line. Stark managed to twist himself
around far enough to see that Gerrith was all right. Her
face was white, her eyes large and strange.

The man-at-arms used his lance again, this time with
less force, to straighten his prisoner in the saddle. Stark
shook away the last of the haze from his vision and tried
to ignore the throbbing in his head. Amnir was riding
up to him.

There was something peculiar about the man's expression as he looked at Stark. It was plain that the en-
counter with the men of the Towers had shaken him.

"So," said Stark, "you meant us for the Citadel all
along."

"Does that surprise you?"

"No. But the Corn King surprised me."

"The what?"

"The man you called Hargoth, the priest-king of the

Towers. He knew me. He was waiting. That's why we were being watched."

"You will get little good from that," said Amnir, and turned to the man-at-arms. "See that he's put into the wagon. Now. And guarded well."

"Guarded against what?" asked Stark. "The People of the Towers? Can you guard against magicians? Or the Thyrans. Perhaps they'd prefer to sell us to the Citadel themselves, without sharing the profits. Or the Lords Protector. Suppose they see no reason to pay you the price you've been rolling under your tongue ever since Kazimni talked to you in Izvand. Suppose they send their Northhounds to hunt us all down." Stark laughed, a small unpleasant sound. "Or are you perhaps beginning, in spite of yourself, to think that there may be something in the wise woman's prophecy? If that's it, hurry, Amnir! See if you can outrun fate."

Amnir's eyelids flickered uneasily. He said something Stark could not hear, probably a curse, and rode away, kicking his beast with unnecessary viciousness.

Stark was put into the wagon and bound with even more care than usual. He lay staring up at the tilt of the rough canvas above him, hearing again the Corn King's words. *The star-roads are open. We have waited through the long night and now it is morning.*

Old Sun's pale gleaming had long since vanished from the canvas when the wagon was wheeled into place for the night. Stark lay still, feeling a curious and quite unfounded anticipation. He listened to the sounds of Amnir's men making camp. He listened to the fretting of the wind at the canvas. He listened to the beating of his own heart. And he waited.

I have seen it in the Winter Dreaming. I have seen it in the entrails of the Spring Child. Our guide has come—

The noises of the camp died away. The men had eaten and wrapped themselves for sleep, all but the sentries. There seemed to be more of them than usual, from the number of pacing feet. From time to time one of the guards looked in through the flap, making sure that the prisoner was still safely bound.

Time went by.

Perhaps I was wrong, Stark thought. Perhaps nothing at all will happen.

He had no clear idea what he was waiting for. A sudden attack, the swift rush of footsteps, shouts, cries— The watchers sent out by the Corn King had had no difficulty keeping up with the slow-moving wagons, and the People of the Towers ought to be able to come up with the train at some time during the night.

And suppose they did come; suppose they did attack. Amnir's men were disciplined and well armed. They were on guard. Could the People of the Towers overcome them? What weapons did they have? How well did they fight?

If they were truly great magicians, they would have more subtle ways of gaining their ends. But were they, truly?

He did not know. And he began at length to think that he would never know.

The cold, he thought, was more penetrating than usual. It pinched his face. He worried about frostbite and tried to burrow his nose deeper into his sleeping furs, one side at a time. The moisture of his own breath froze upon the furs, upon his flesh and hair. His lungs hurt. He grew drowsy, and he could picture himself asleep and freezing gradually into a statue with a shining glaze of ice over him like glass.

He was afraid.

He fought his bonds. He did not break free, but he generated enough heat to melt some of the frost that had gathered around him.

It froze again, and now he could *hear* the cold.

It sang. Each crystal of ice had a voice, tiny and thin.

It tinkled and crackled, faintly, sweetly, like distant music heard across hills when the wind blows.

It chimed, and the chiming spoke elfinly of sleep and peace. Peace, and an end of striving.

All living things must come to that at last.

Surrender to sleep and peace.

Stark was still fighting feebly against that temptation when the back flap of the wagon-tilt opened and a narrow person came lithely in over the tailgate. Moving swiftly, he slashed Stark's wrists and ankles free. He hauled him up, amazingly strong for all his narrowness, and forced a draught of some dark liquid down Stark's throat.

"Come," he said. "Quickly."

The face, masked in plain gray without markings, swam in the gloom, unreal. Stark pawed his way forward, and the draught he had drunk took sudden fire within him. He half climbed, half fell out of the wagon. The strong arm of the gray man steadied him.

Inside the circle of wagons the tiny hoarded fires guttered behind their windbreaks, dying. Bodies, animal and human, lay about, motionless under a shining coat of frost that shone pale in the starlight. The sentries lay where they had fallen, awkward things like dummies with uplifted arms and stiffly contracted legs.

Stark articulated one word. "Gerrith."

The gray man pointed and urged him on.

The Corn King stood on a small eminence beyond the camp. Behind him, a number of lesser priests were spaced along the line of a wide semicircle. It was as if they formed a drawn bow, with the Corn King at the tip of the arrow. They were all quite motionless, their masked faces bent upon the camp. Stark's guide took good care not to pass in front of that silent bow and arrow. He led Stark off to one side. The deadly cold relaxed its grip.

Stark said again, "Gerrith."

The gray man turned toward the camp. Two figures came stumbling from the wagons, one narrow and masked and supporting the other, clad in furs. When they came closer Stark saw a thick swinging braid of hair and knew that the fur-clad one was Gerrith.

He exhaled a breath of relief that steamed on the icy air. Then he said, "Where are the others?"

The gray man did not answer. Stark grasped him by one thin sinewy shoulder and shook him. "Where are the others?"

The Corn King's voice spoke behind him. The semi-circle was broken; the work of the arrow done.

"We have no need of them," the Corn King said. "The Sun Woman I have use for. The others are worthless."

"Nevertheless," said Stark quietly, "I will have them. Now. And safe. Also, we will need arms."

Hargoth hesitated, his eyes catching a glint of starlight so the holes in his mask gleamed eerily. Then he shrugged and sent four of his people running back to the wagons.

"It will do no harm," he said, "nor any good, either. Your friends will die later on, and less kindly, that is all."

Stark looked toward the camp and at the still figures on the ground. "What did you do to them?"

"I sent the Holy Breath of the Goddess upon them." He made a sign in the air. "My Lady Cold. She will give them sleep, and the everlasting peace."

So that was the end of Amnir and his energetic greed. Stark found it difficult to feel much pity for him. The men-at-arms were doing a dangerous job for their living, but he felt little sympathy for them, either. His wrists and ankles bore the scars of their hospitality.

Hargoth indicated a long, low ridge, a fold in the plain. "My folk have made camp beyond. There is fire. We have food and drink. Come."

Stark shook his head. "Not until I see our comrades."

They stood, in the biting air, until Halk and Breca and the brothers had been brought, together with weapons borrowed from the dead. Then they followed the Corn King toward the ridge.

"There is food in those wagons," said Halk. He walked crookedly, having been bound for many days. Some of the strength had gone out of him, but he was as belligerent as ever, perhaps worse because he was conscious of his weakness. "Are you going to leave it all there for whatever beasts there are in this wilderness?"

"We do not need it," said Hargoth. "And we are not thieves. Whatever is in the wagons belongs to the Thyrans."

"Then why not us?"

"You were no part of their bargain with the trader."

Stark steadied Gerrith over a stretch of bare rock. "You said that word had come to you from the high north. Who sent that word?"

"The Wandsmen. They told us to watch for strangers coming from the south. They offered a high price for you."

"But you do not intend to take it?"

"No."

"Why not?"

"There was other news from the high north. A man not of this world has been brought to the Citadel. The Harsenyi nomads saw him with the Wandsmen in the passes of the Bleak Mountains. The Wandsmen like to hide their secrets but the Harsenyi see everything. They range over half the world, and they carry news." The Corn King glanced sidelong at Stark. "Besides, there is the Sight, and I knew who you were when my people first saw you riding beside the wagons. You are not of this world. You come from the south, and it is said that there is a place in the south where the starships land. The Harsenyi brought this word from Izvand."

"It is true," said Stark.

"Ah," said Hargoth. "I saw it clearly, in the Winter Dreaming. The ships stand like bright towers beside the sea."

They had reached the crest of the ridge. Below, somewhat sheltered from the wind, Stark saw the fires, and the humped shapes of skin tents already dusted with snow.

"That is where we wish to go," said Hargoth. "That is why we will not sell you to the Wandsmen. You will lead us, to the stars."

He bent his head humbly before Stark. But his eyes, looking upward, were not humble.

15

Stark walked halfway down the slope, so that Hargoth was obliged to follow. Then he stopped.

"I will lead you," he said, "after we have taken the Citadel. Not before."

The wind moaned against the ridge, sending a frozen spindrift of white crystals across it that drifted down on Stark and the Irnanese, on Hargoth and his lesser priests. There was an instinctive movement, each group gathering apart from the other. After that, they stood very still.

Hargoth said, "The ships are in the south."

Stark nodded. "Unfortunately, that gate is shut. There is war in the south. Other men beside you wish to follow those star-roads, and the Wandsmen are saying they cannot. They are killing, in the name of the Lords Protector. The only way to open that gate is to take the Citadel, destroy the Lords Protector, and the Wandsmen along with them. Otherwise, you will go south only to die."

The wind moaned and the fine white spindrift fell.

Hargoth turned to Gerrith. "Sun Woman, is this all true?"

"It is true," she answered.

"Besides," said Stark, suddenly very weary of trying to cope with people who stubbornly insisted on getting in his way, "if Skaith were an open world, certain kinds of ships could land anywhere on the planet instead of being confined to the enclave at Skeg. There would be no need for your people to go south. It would be much easier for ships to come to you."

Hargoth did not answer this. Stark had no idea what he might be thinking. He was only certain of one thing, that he would not be taken captive again by anyone if he had to die fighting. He shifted his weight slightly, wishing that his muscles were not quite so stiff with cold.

"You are wise in your knowledge," Hargoth said at last. "What shall I call you?"

"Stark."

"You are wise in your own knowledge, Stark, but I am wise in mine. And I tell you that Thyra lies between us and the Citadel."

"Is there no way around? The land seems broad enough."

"Until it narrows. Thyra bestrides that narrowness. Thyra is strong and populous. And greedy." He paused, and then added harshly, "They have dealings with the Wandsmen. The same word that came to us would have come even sooner to them."

Stark nodded. He stared at the ground, scowling.

"South," said Hargoth. "That is the only way."

His voice held an inflexible note of triumph. Stark kept his peace, answering only with a shrug, into which Hargoth could read any meaning that pleased him.

Apparently he read acquiescence, because he turned and started down the slope. "The fires are warm, the shelters are ready. Let us enjoy them. Tomorrow, at his rising, we will ask a blessing of Old Sun."

Stark perforce followed Hargoth this time. There was nothing of menace in what the man had said, yet Stark felt a twinge of unease. He looked at Gerrith, walking beside him with the long braid swinging. Sun-colored braid beneath the frost. Sun-colored woman. What did Hargoth want of her?

He was about to speak to Gerrith. But she gave him a warning look, and then Hargoth glanced over his shoulder at them, giving them a sharp-edged smile.

Blank-faced, they followed him down.

The folk in the camp were all young men. Women,

children, and older men, they were told, were already making preparations for the migration, packing the belongings, dismantling the homes in the broken towers, drying meat and making journey-bread, choosing the beasts that would be saved from the present slaughter to support them later on.

They were singing, said Hargoth, the very ancient hymn preserved from times beyond remembrance, taught once in each lifetime but never sung until now. The Hymn of Deliverance.

> *The Promised One shall lead us*
> *Down the long roads of the stars,*
> *Toward a new beginning . . .*

The men sang it around the fires as Stark and the others came in. Their faces were flushed, their eyes brilliant, fixed upon this stranger from the far places of heaven. Stark felt embarrassed and more than a little annoyed. Ever since he had landed on Skaith people had been forcing shackles on him, shackles of duty that he had not himself chosen and did not want. Damn these people and their prophecies and legends!

"Our forefathers were men of knowledge," said Hargoth. "They dreamed of star-flight. While the world died around them they continued to dream, and to work, but it was too late. They left with us the promise that, though we could not go, one day you would come to us."

Stark was glad when the hymn ended.

Gerrith refused food and asked to be shown to her shelter, alone. Her face had that remote prophetess look on it. Stark saw the skin flaps of the tent fall shut behind her with a feeling of chill between his shoulder-blades.

He ate the food that was given him, not because he was especially hungry but because the hunting animal never knows how long it may be until the next meal. He drank the strong drink that seemed to be made of fermented milk. The Irnanese sat near him in a close group. He sensed that they wanted to talk but were inhibited by Hargoth and his people, who crouched or moved among the fires like slender ghosts with their high stooping shoulders and their gray-masked faces all alike and without expression. Despite the fact that the People of the Towers had rescued them from Amnir's shackles, Stark did not like them. There was a touch of madness in them, born of the long dark and the too-long-held faith. It made him feel no easier that their madness was centered on him.

The flaps of Gerrith's tent opened. She came and stood in the firelight. She had thrown off her heavy outer garments, and her head was bare. In her hands she held the small ivory skull, still speckled with the slaughter of Irnan.

Hargoth had risen. Gerrith faced him, and her eyes meeting his were like two copper sunrays meeting ice.

She spoke, and her voice rang sweet and clear as it had that day when Mordach tried to shame her and died for it.

"Hargoth," she said. "You intend to give me to Old Sun as a gift, to buy his blessing."

Hargoth did not look aside, though he must have heard Stark and the Irnanese getting to their feet, clapping hands to weapons.

"Yes," he said to Gerrith, "you are a chosen sacrifice, sent to me for that purpose."

Gerrith shook her head. "It is not my fate to die here, and if you kill me you and your people will never walk the star-roads nor see a brighter sun."

Her voice carried such conviction that Hargoth hesitated over whatever words he had been about to say.

"My place is with the Promised One," said Gerrith. "My path lies northward. And I tell you there will be blood and enough to feed Old Sun before this is finished."

She held the skull higher in her two hands, over the

fire, and the flames turned a sullen red, staining them all with the color of death.

Now Hargoth looked uncertain. But he was proud and obstinate. "I am king," he said. "And high priest. I know what must be done for my people."

"Do you?" asked Stark quietly. "Can you be sure? You know only the dream. I am reality. How do you know that I am truly the Promised One?"

"You come from the stars," said Hargoth.

"Yes. But so does the stranger who was brought to the Citadel, and he is the one who tells the ships to come, not I."

Hargoth stared at him for a long moment in the red glare of the fire.

"He has that power?"

"He has," said Stark. "How can you be sure that *he* is not the Promised One?"

Gerrith lowered her hands and stepped back from the fire. The flames returned to their normal color. She said calmly, "You stand at the crossroads, Hargoth. The path you choose now will determine the fate of your people."

A heavy and sententious statement, Stark thought, but he felt no desire to smile at it. It was the simple truth, and it involved his own and Ashton's fate as well as that of Hargoth's people.

His hand closed over the hilt of the sword taken from one of Amnir's men. He waited for Hargoth's answer. If the stupid man insisted on sacrificing Gerrith and going south, Old Sun was going to have some victims here and now.

Hargoth's gaze flicked uncertainly between Stark and Gerrith—the chill, flat, shining gaze of madness, of fanatic conviction. The lesser priests who had assisted him at Amnir's camp were gathered nearby, their masked faces immobile, watching. Suddenly Hargoth turned on his heel and joined them. They went apart. Their backs formed a wall that hid whatever they might be doing, but the movement of their shoulders indicated that some sort of ritual was being performed. They chanted, a low sonorous murmuring.

"Lacking a live victim," Gerrith said, "they're consulting some other augury."

"It had better be favorable," said Halk, and drew his swordblade hissing from the sheath.

The silence lengthened. The guttering fire hissed as snow and frost fell into it. The People of the Towers stood in the blowing darkness beyond, and waited.

The priests made one long moaning sigh. They bowed to some invisible Presence. Then they returned to the fire.

"Three times we have cast the sacred finger-bones of the Spring Child," said Hargoth. "Three times, they pointed north." His eyes showed a desperate, thwarted rage. "Very well. We will go up against the Thyrans. And if we win past them, do you know what waits beyond Thyra, to keep us from the Citadel?"

"Yes," said Stark, "I know. The Northhounds."

A shadow crossed Gerrith's face. She shivered.

"What is it?" asked Stark.

"I don't know. It seemed—that when you spoke that name, one heard it."

Across the desolate miles to the north, a great white shape had paused in its measured padding through blowing snow. It turned and swung a huge, fanged muzzle southward, questing across the wind.

16

As Hargoth had said, the broad land narrowed. It began to rise sharply toward a series of ridges, and on either hand were rough hills and deep gullies choked with tumbled ice. The track of Amnir's wagons still followed the ancient road. Apparently the summer thaw was strong enough to cut the road in many places. It had been remade across the beds of wider channels, the narrower ones filled in with stones, a tribute to the hard work and enterprise of Amnir's men. And much good it had done them in the end.

With Hargoth's people, the party now numbered thirty-six: two tens of fighting men and their captain, armed with slings and javelins; the Corn King and eight priests, armed with magic; and the original six from Irnan, counting Stark, who would just as soon have dispensed with his new allies. The force was too large to move easily in secret, and too small to be effective as an attack unit. Still, he thought the Corn King and his priests might be useful in one way, when they came to meet the Northhounds. The breath of the Goddess might at least slow down these legendary demons. In any case, he had had no choice.

The narrow men in gray proved to be nearly tireless. Their marching gait was a sort of springy trot that was difficult at first for Stark and the others to keep up with after the long days of captivity. But they fell into the pace gradually, feeling strength and elasticity returning. Only Halk, who had suffered the worst confinement, stumbled along at the rear, sweating and cursing. He was so vile-tempered that Breca gave up trying to help him and rejoined the others.

"How far to Thyra?" asked Stark.

"Three long marches." Hargoth had not been to Thyra himself, but Kintoth, captain of the fighting men, had. He wore lightning-strokes on the cheeks of his mask and he carried an iron sword.

"We go there somewhiles to trade for tools and weapons," Kintoth said, slapping his sword-hilt. "The Thyrans are great smiths. We always go in force. We trade them dried meat as well as hides and cloth, but in the old days before the trader we were afraid of being added to their foodstocks ourselves. Now that Amnir is dead, we shall have to start worrying again. The Thyrans keep beasts and trade knives to the lichen-gatherers for fodder but there's never enough in the starving times."

"We trade women, too," said Hargoth. "A matter of necessity, though neither we nor the Thyrans like it. We must both have fresh blood to survive. There was a third city once that neighbored us, but the people kept too fiercely to themselves and finally they died."

He trotted on for some time in silence. Then he added, "Sometimes the Wandsmen bring us women from the south. They don't live long here. Usually we give them to Old Sun." And he looked at Gerrith.

"What about the Citadel?" asked Stark, not missing the look.

"We've never seen it. No one has. Not even the Harsenyi. There are the Northhounds, to guard against strangers. And there is the mist."

"Mist?"

"Thick mist that boils like steam above a cauldron and never lifts. It is a strong magic. The Citadel is always hidden."

"But you know the way there?"

"I know what the Harsenyi have said. Some of their people serve the Wandsmen."

"But you don't really know. Do the Thyrans?"

"I have told you. The way is known, and not known."

"What about the women from the south?"

"The ones they give us are never taken to the Citadel, but brought straight on." Hargoth's mouth was a thin line. "The gifts of the Wandsmen! They bring us more than women. Small phials and pretty powders, joy and dreams for all, and perpetual slavery. They tempt our young ones to go south and join the Farers. We are not fond of the Wandsmen."

Hargoth studied the strangers. Old Sun was above the horizon now, and his gaze moved from one face to another, not hurrying, seeing in the rusty daylight what he had not seen by starlight or by the flickering gleam of the fires.

"You have come a long way to destroy them. Why?"

They told him.

Hargoth listened. When they had finished he said, "You Southrons must be soft indeed to let yourselves be so badly ruled."

Gerrith held up a hand to forestall Halk's angry outburst. She looked coldly at Hargoth and said, "You've heard of the Farers. You've never seen them. You've never seen a mob in action. Perhaps you will before you're through. Tell me your opinion then."

Hargoth inclined his head.

"The Lords Protector," Stark said. "What do you know of them?"

"I think they're a lie, told to keep the Wandsmen in power. Or if they ever lived, they've been dead a thousand years. That's why I would call this a fool's errand, except that I know the Wandsmen are real. And if, as you say, they intend to keep us from the stars—."

Apparently he was still not quite convinced. And he continued to glance sidelong at Gerrith from time to time, in a manner that Stark did not care for.

"My lord Darkness, my lady Cold, and their daughter Hunger," Stark said. "You worship the Goddess and she sends her power through you. Yet you also worship Old Sun?"

"We need him to keep the darker gods at bay. Otherwise we would die. Besides, the Sun Woman was to be a parting gift."

Long after Old Sun's setting they went aside from the road and found a secure hollow in the hills. The warriors built tiny fires of what dead mosses and lichens they could find among the wind-scoured stones. They had not expected to be so long away from the Towers and so the rations were short. No one complained. They were all used to hunger.

When it was time to crawl into the skin tents for sleep, Stark said to Gerrith, "You'll shelter with me. I think Hargoth still has notions."

She accepted that without protest. Stark saw Halk watching, wise and sneering, as he followed Gerrith into the tent.

Their two bodies crowded the small space, and Stark realized that this was the first time since that bloody day in the square of Irnan that he had been alone with Gerrith. On the way to Izvand there had been the Irnanese and the troop of mercenaries, and not so much as a hand's breadth of privacy. Halk and Breca pleasured themselves as the fancy took them, without embarrassment, but theirs was an old relationship. Stark and Gerrith had no relationship beyond their two roles as Wise Woman and Dark Man, one hardly conducive to intimacy, and he was not at all sure that she wanted any other. Her status as prophetess set her apart, surrounding her with a certain aura of untouchability. Besides, it had been most hellishly cold.

Afterward, as Amnir's captives, they had had no opportunity even for conversation, let alone anything else.

Now, in the shelter, with a minuscule lamp for light and each other for warmth, he felt something totally new. He was conscious that they touched, at thigh and hip and shoulder. Their breath mingled in faint clouds of vapor. Animal heat rose from their living flesh. Lying close, he felt her stop shivering, and he put his hand on hers.

"Has your gift told you yet why it was you had to come all this weary way?"

"Let's not talk about it now." She turned her head and looked at him. "Let's not talk about anything now."

He drew her to him. She smiled and did not resist. With his fingertips he traced the outline of her cheek and jaw; thin, he noticed, with the beautiful structure of the bones quite clear beneath the wind-browned skin. Her eyes were enormous, her mouth soft and sweet, welcoming.

He kissed her, a first tentative touching of the lips, and her arms came around him fiercely, and after that nothing was tentative. She was strong and hungry, warm life in that place of cold and death, giving and taking without stint. And Stark knew that this had been going to happen right from the beginning, from the moment when Mordach ripped away the robe and left her clothed in nothing but her magnificent and indestructible pride.

Neither of them spoke of love. Love is for a long future. They slept in each other's arms and were content.

In the black morning they were away again, following the green star. They halted briefly for the ritual greeting of Old Sun at his rising, when Hargoth looked regretfully at Gerrith, who was surrounded by Stark and the Irnanese. At noon they halted a second time to rest and chew their journey rations, hard chunks of edible lichens pressed into cakes and a strong-flavored mixture of fat and meat fibers pounded together with bitter herbs.

Stark discussed strategy with Kintoth.

"You see here," said the captain, making out a rough map in the snow with his finger. "This is the road we're on now. It winds about so, and here is Thyra, sitting on a dozen hills. The old city, that is. The new one is dug in

and around." His finger made vague marks on the peri-
meter.

"How old is the new city?" asked Stark.

"Not as old as ours. No. Say only a thousand years,
or so. The People of the Hammer came out of nowhere,
the bards tell us, and took up these ancient cities . . ."

"More than one?"

"There are several tribes. The Thyrans are the only
ones we have to do with, but it is said that there are
more in other places, and that they all have the same
god, Strayer of the Forges."

"They all have the same madness," said Hargoth,
"and that madness is for iron and the working of it.
They mine the bones of the cities, and the metal is more
than wealth to them, it is life."

"All right." Stark looked at the map. "The road.
Thyra, old and new. What else?"

Kintoth sketched stylized mountains on the far side of
Thyra. "These are called the Witchfires, for a reason
you will understand when you see them. They mark the
boundary between the darklands and the high north.
Here is the pass that we must take to cross them, if we
ever reach it."

Thyra stood like a wall before the mouth of the pass.

"Is there no other way across the mountains?"

Kintoth shrugged. "There may be a hundred. This is
the only one we know, and the Citadel lies somewhere
beyond it. Now, on the road, here . . ." He drew fortifica-
tions across the approach to Thyra. "This post is strongly held. And all around the city are sentry posts." His
finger poked random little holes in the snow. "I don't
know the exact locations. The Thyrans live in and
around the edges of the ruins, and they're more vulnerable than we in the Towers. They take care to guard their
wealth and their precious flesh, lest both be devoured."

The land seemed totally deserted. Stark asked, "What
enemies have they here?"

"This is the northern edge of the darklands," said

Hargoth. "We live all our lives in a state of siege. Anyone, anything, may come. Sometimes the great snowdragons, with the frost white on their wings and their hungry teeth showing. Sometimes a band of Outdwellers who run demented across the world and take whatever they can lay claws on. And there are creatures who wait, hidden just out of sight, smelling the warm food that walks and hoping they can snatch it."

"It doesn't do to show weakness or inattention," said Kintoth. "The Harsenyi, for instance, might be tempted to attack if they thought they could gain by it. The other tribes of the Hammer might become greedy. And of course, the Thyrans have a bigger worry than most."

He stabbed his finger at the sketched-in range of the Witchfires. "They have neighbors here among the mountains. The Children of Skaith-Our-Mother."

Stark stared at him in the brassy twilight of the hollow. The wind blew snow in vagrant clouds.

Halk laughed, a harsh and jarring sound.

"Perhaps you will be lucky a second time, Dark Man!" he said, and laughed again.

17

Shadows lay long across the road, pointing north. Soft-shod, the party moved quietly. Wind scoured, their tracks faded away as soon as they were made.

"What are they like, these Children of Skaith-Our-Mother?"

Hargoth shook his narrow head. "The Thyrans say they're monsters. They have many tales of them, all horrible."

"Are they true?"

"Who can say?"

"You have no knowledge yourself? Haven't any of your people gone into the mountains? Through the pass?"

"In the darklands," said Hargoth, "it is difficult enough to stay where one is. One does not travel for any reason other than survival."

"The Harsenyi seem to manage it."

"They're nomads, it's their way of life. They're strong enough to fight off the brainless attackers, the hungry mouths, and the rest of us thank them. They're the only link we have with the outer world. They bring things we haven't got and can't make, and most of all they bring news. Being nomads, they don't compete with us for food and shelter. Besides, we're used to them."

"And they cross the Witchfires."

"And more. It is said that they even trade with the Hooded Men on the far side of the Bleak Mountains." He paused, considering. "It is *said* that they trade with the Children of Skaith."

Stark kept his voice free of irritation, though with an

effort. "And what do the Harsenyi say of the Children?"

"That they are monsters, and greater magicians than we. That they have power over stones and all things belonging to the ground, which they can cause to shake whenever they wish. They say—"

"They say. The Harsenyi are doubtless the fount of all wisdom, except that traders have been known to lie before now in order to keep their markets secret. Does anybody know?"

"If you mean, can I give you firm knowledge of the Children—no, I cannot."

"You're trying to talk them away, Dark Man," said Halk. "They will not go so easily."

Stark glanced at him, but did not bother to reply. He wondered if he looked as trail-worn and hollow-eyed as did Halk and the others. The sturdy furs bought at Izvand had turned mangy with use, showing bare spots where the thongs had rubbed. The men had stopped shaving, perforce, since Amnir had allowed them nothing in the way of knives or razors. Since their release they had been content to enjoy beards and longer hair as a protection against the cold. The women covered their faces with wrappings against the cold. Breca walked steadily beside Halk. Gerrith, now, walked beside Stark, and her eyes smiled. She alone seemed alive, here and now. The rest were like automatons, waiting for someone to press the buttons.

Stark felt much the same way himself. Land and sky lay upon him like a burden: cold, empty, without promise.

And no one knew what had happened in the south.

The shadows lengthened. The wind blew down from the high north, skirling dry snow.

They came to a place, and Kintoth caught Stark's arm. "There! See there? In the sky, Stark. Look up!"

Stark looked, and saw a glitter and dazzle of pale gold.

"Those are the Witchfires."

The peaks disappeared again as the road bent.

Two of Kintoth's men who had gone ahead as scouts came racing back down the road, loping like grey-hounds.

"A party, coming from Thyra."

"How large?" asked Kintoth.

"Large. We saw them only from a distance."

In a few moments they were off the road, settling themselves among the rocks and hollows. Stark left it to Kintoth to make sure there were no betraying marks. He found himself a vantage point where he could overlook the road. Halk lay down beside him. A short distance away Hargoth watched and waited, and presently Kintoth joined him.

The Thyrans were audible a long way off. Drums beat a steady marching pace, accompanied by the inter-mittent squealing of some shrill-voiced instrument and the clashing of metal on metal. After a while the party came round a bend in the road.

Stark estimated the Thyrans at half a hundred men, including pipers and drummers and cymbal-clashers. All were armed with iron weapons. All wore iron caps, and iron-studded back- and breast-plates over their furs. Iron-bound targes were slung behind the left shoulder. Banners and pennons lashed in the wind above them, barred scarlet and black, with the device of a hammer. They were short broad men who had a look of power about them, and they marched with a driving purpose-fulness that had in it something chilling, like the march of army ants. They were not, one felt, accustomed to de-feat.

Behind the soldiers came a party of unarmed men hauling iron-framed carts loaded with supplies.

"They'll be going to meet the trader," said Halk, low-voiced even though the drumming and clashing would have drowned any other sound. "I wish them joy when they find him."

Stark waited until the last clanking cart had vanished along the road, and then he went to Hargoth.

"Do the Thyrans send out an escort every year for the trader?"

"No. We keep watch for large parties of armed men."

"That is so," said Kintoth. "Once or twice we've watched the trader almost to the gates of Thyra, and they've had no more than the usual lookouts. There's no way of telling just when the wagons may come, and anyway, Amnir had a force sufficient for his safety."

"Nevertheless," said Stark, "Halk thinks that's where they're going." He pondered. "Could they be going to attack, say, the Towers?"

"Not with fifty men. I'd say Halk's right."

"Yet as you say, Amnir had a force sufficient for his safety. This force is large enough to overcome, or at least overawe, Amnir's force. It looks as if they have a very special interest in the trader this year, perhaps connected with something he might have that the Thyrans might want to take away from him—something of unusual value. I wonder if the Thyrans have had some late word from the Citadel about us."

"We were undoubtedly followed to Izvand," said Gerrith. "Fast messengers could have taken word up the Wandsmen's road that Amnir left there in search of us."

"Fast or slow, it makes no difference," said Halk. "We'll never get past Thyra anyway unless we can make ourselves a new road."

"We start on that right now," said Stark. The old road had suddenly become menacing. There might be any number of patrols and lookout posts. Stark tried to calculate how long it would take the armed escort to find whatever was left of Amnir and his wagon-train, and get word of the disaster back to Thyra. Presumably they would send a runner. And then what? Would the Thyrans start scouring the hills?

He reckoned they had better be through the Witch-fires as quickly as possible.

They struck away from the old track. It was not difficult to keep direction. Old Sun smeared the southwestern sky with dull red-ochre, and when that had faded the green star shone hugely, almost as bright as a little moon, in the northeast. Stark depended on Kintoth to tell him where Thyra ought to be. The going was by turns fairly easy, and very rough, and often the way was barred completely by a sheer cliff or an impassable gorge. This made for weary backtracking. Progress was discouragingly slow.

There was no love-making that night. They did not stop at all except when weariness forced them to, and then only until enough strength returned to let them go on again. There was no complaint, even from Halk. They all seemed to feel that the hills were dangerous, too dangerous for peaceful rest, and they were anxious to be out of them.

The Lamp of the North climbed higher. The aurora, brilliant in the sky, flared white and rose-pink and ice-green. And there was a new presence in the night.

The peaks of the Witchfires stood tall in the north. They caught these delicate colors on their ice-sheathed flanks and sent them gleaming and glimmering back in flashes of many-faceted light, a wonder born of the cold.

"The Witchfires are sacred to the Goddess," said Hargoth, "though we see them seldom."

Along toward midnight, Stark found a trail.

18

It was a furtive, cunning sort of trail, such as animals make, and it was only because Stark had lived his life in the wild places that he saw it at all. The trail was going the way he wanted to go and so he decided to follow it for the time being. It was very narrow, sliding up and down the slopes, twisting cleverly to avoid the cliffs and canyons. After a while he realized that it was not a single trail but one of a network of footways through the hills.

He asked who might have made them, and Hargoth said, "Outdwellers, probably, though other beings may use it. Cities attract them, as I told you. There is always the hope of food."

It was impossible to tell if the trail had been recently used. The bare ground was frozen too hard, and where the snow lay there was no sign of prints. If there had been any, the wind or some other agency had wiped them out.

Stark went ahead of the party, trusting to no one but himself.

He caught a taint of smoke in the clean air. Going more cautiously, he saw a ridge ahead. Sounds came from beyond the ridge. Unbelievable sounds.

He went back to warn the others, then crept on his belly up to the top of the ridge.

He looked down into a shallow bowl between the hills. A fire of dead lichen burned small at one side, within a ring of blackened stones. The tiny flickering it made was no more than a pinpoint. The bowl brimmed with the light of the aurora and the green star. The

Witchfires sparkled against the north. Snow covering the slopes of the bowl sparkled more faintly, and in that shadowless gleaming a score of figures danced to the wild thin music of a reedy pipe.

They danced in a wide circle, moving widdershins round the slopes. They leapt and whirled, and when they did so they laughed and their tatters flew: the height and the lightness of their leaping, and the grace and the swift rushing joy of it made them seem to take wing upon outstretched arms. Joyousness, Stark thought, was a rare thing anywhere, and he had seen little of it on Skaith. But this was a curious place in which to find it.

There was no set pattern to their dancing, except that they kept the circle. Now and again two or more would join together and go skittering hand in hand, with the laughter spilling out of them in long trills like birdsong, to caper about the piper, who leapt and whirled by himself in the center of the dance. Sometimes he would do a contral-step with them, and sometimes he would do a circle of his own, clockwise against the circle's turning.

After a while it seemed to Stark that there was something more than joy in their frolicking. A certain quality. What was the word Hargoth had used? Demented?

He turned as someone slid softly up beside him. He could see the twin lightning strokes on the mask. Kintoth peered over the ridge and then drew back.

"Outdwellers," he said.

Stark nodded. "They seem to know every inch of these hills. Perhaps they know of a way around Thyra."

"It's worth a try," said Kintoth, "but remember, they're an unchancy lot. Don't turn your back on them, even for a moment." He added, "And remember, the Wandsmen may have spoken to them about you."

"That had occurred to me," Stark said. "Tell the others to come up and stand along here, where they can be seen. Weapons ready."

Kintoth hurried away. Stark waited a moment or two. Then he rose and began to walk down the slope.

He could not say who saw him first. But the piping wavered away, and the dancing stilled. The dark figures stood quietly in the beautiful shining from the sky. They watched him, not speaking, and their tatters ruffled in the wind like feathers.

Stark gave them the formal greeting. "May Old Sun bring you warmth and life."

One of the Outdwellers came forward. It was a woman, he thought. They were a thin people, with wild locks hanging under curious little caps, and their coverings were not revealing. The coverings, he saw now, were made of many small skins sewed together, and the tatters were the legs and tails flapping free. The woman's face was narrow and pale, with a pointed chin and enormous eyes that slanted upward. There were no whites to the eyes, only irises of lambent green with hugely expanded pupils that seemed to reflect the night entire.

"Old Sun is well enough," she said carelessly. Her accent was strange, difficult to follow, and her mouth was strange too, with exceedingly sharp protruding teeth. "We worship the Dark Goddess. May the night bring you life and joy."

Stark hoped that it would. He did not count on it. "Who is your leader here?"

"Leader?" She cocked her head on one side. "We have all sorts. What's your fancy? A leader for singing the clouds and stars, a leader for catching the wind and one for setting it free again, a leader . . ."

"One for the making of trails," said Stark. "I wish to pass by Thyra, unseen."

"Ah," she said, and looked past him over his shoulder, to the rim of the bowl. "You alone? Or with these others I see: Gray Warlocks of the Towers and five persons unknown."

"All of us."

"Unseen?"

"Yes."

"And unheard?"

"Of course."

"But you are not as fleet as we, nor as light of foot. We can go where a snowflake would be heard, and it falling."

"Nonetheless," said Stark, "we will try."

She turned to her people. "The strangers and the Gray Ones would pass by Thyra in secret. Slaifed?" She sang the name.

A man came to her, laughing, kicking the dry snow. "I will lead them." They were a small people, these night-dancers, the tallest of them reaching no higher than Stark's shoulders. Slaifed looked him up and down and across and made a rude sound. "I can do that, but I can't make your great hoofs be silent. That is up to you."

"And their weapons," said the woman. "Don't forget their weapons."

"No one forgets weapons," said Slaifed, and laughed again, a peculiarly lilting sound that somehow sent a shiver across Stark's nerves. Slaifed himself bore no weapons, at least none that Stark could see, except for a knife such as everyone carried for the necessities of daily life.

"Follow me," said the Outdweller, "if you can."

He went gusting away across the snow, seeming to ride the wind. The others of his tribe returned to their dancing, all but the woman, who came with Stark. The thin voice of the pipe was audible for some time, fading slowly with distance.

Hargoth's people and the Irnanese went very quickly, in spite of Slaifed's doubting. They went with their hands on their weapons and their eyes alert.

The scarecrow figure of the Outdweller flitted ahead. The Witchfires gleamed and glittered under the shaking aurora.

The woman looked up sidelong at Stark. "You are from the south."

"Yes."

"From the south, and not from the south." She circled him, her small nose lifted. She walked backward, studying the Irnanese. "*They* are from the south. They smell of Skaith." She turned to Stark again. "Not you. You smell of the dust of heaven and the sacred night."

Stark was not aware that he smelled of anything except a lack of soap and water. But he did not miss the significance of the remark . . . unless the Outdwellers were clairvoyant. He said, "You're given to fancies, little sister." His gaze roved constantly over Slaifed, the trail, the ever-shifting hills. The piping had ceased now, perhaps because it was too far away to be heard. "How are you called?"

"Slee," she said. "Slee-e-e-e . . . like the wind running over a hill."

"Were you always wanderers, Slee?"

"Since the beginning. Our people have never had roofs to prison them. All this is ours." Her wide arms touched everything, hills and sky, the Witchfires, the darklands behind them. "In the time of the Great Wandering we were the free plunderers who fed on the roof-dwellers."

Stark thought that probably she meant that quite literally. She was proud of it. She danced with pride, going a little ahead of him. Slaifed was even farther ahead. This part of the trail was fairly straight, with a steep hillside on the right and a sharp drop-off to the left, into a ravine with a frozen stream at the bottom. The hillside could be climbed at need, but not easily.

A hundred feet or so on, the trail bent around a jutting shoulder of rock. Suddenly Slaifed began to run.

So did Slee.

So did Stark.

Slee's hands were at her breast when Stark caught her and flung her aside with a swinging slash of his hand, never breaking stride. Slaifed looked back, not believing that anyone but an Outdweller could move so swiftly. He reached into the breast of his tunic, still going like the wind.

Stark caught him halfway round the rock. It was like catching a bird. He sank his fingers into the long thin neck that was all cord and muscle, and set his feet, and did a thing that made Slaifed's body snap upward as one snaps a whip.

Stark saw the Outdweller's absolutely incredulous face, saw a double set of iron talons, only half drawn on over thin fingers, drop to the ground. Then he had flung the body against Slee, turning as she came into his back.

Her iron claws were in place and slashing. He felt the metal, still warm from her flesh. Then she fell under Slaifed's dead weight and Stark killed her with one blow. She stared up at him from the white ground, the great dark pupils still reflecting the night, though not so brightly.

The column, headed by the Irnanese, had come to a halt. Weapons were rattling along the line. Stark touched the angle of his jaw where Slee's claws had cut him, two shallow grooves just above the neck. The blood was already beginning to freeze. He drew his sword and went on around the rock.

The trail led straight on, straight to the walls of a Thyran guardpost. There were streaks of light from slitted windows. There were men on the walls and on the squat watchtower. The post filled all the space between the hills and the ravine.

Stark turned back.

Tattered shadows came streaking down the hillside, to leap with outstretched talons onto the marchers. The Outdwellers had decided not to spend the night dancing in the hollow. There was an eruption of noise and violent motion.

Almost at once the harsh bellowing of iron horns sounded from the guardpost.

19

The Outdwellers, inferior in numbers and armament, were relying on their speed and agility. They skittered back and forth and up the hillside out of reach. Kintoth's slingers and javelin-throwers were hampered by the close quarters. They were forced to use the javelins as stabbing weapons, forming a bristling circle around Hargoth and the priests. Kintoth rallied his rear-guard. The Irnanese closed ranks, more dangerous with their swords and spears. The attackers avoided them.

Some few of the Outdwellers fell or were wounded in that first rush, some few of the gray men of the Towers were slashed or forced over the edge of the ravine. That was all. The Outdwellers were fighting a nuisance action, to disrupt the column and hold them for the Thyrans.

Stark joined the Irnanese.

"What's ahead?" asked Halk.

Stark told him.

"How many men?"

"I don't know. But we're in a trap here, we've got to run one way or the other."

"What's behind us but more traps?" said Halk.

"Move, then," said Stark, and ran back along the line, shouting to Kintoth. The men began to move, slowly at first, then more and more rapidly. By the time Stark got back to the head of the column they were going at a run.

They swept around the shoulder of rock and charged headlong into the Thyran soldiers who were coming from the guardpost.

The impact scattered the Thyrans, a dozen or so squat, thick-armed warriors. Stark and the tall Irnanese hewed with the strength of desperation, blades ringing on iron. Kintoth's light-armed troop had a bit more room to work in here and javelins were finding unprotected legs and throats. If this dozen, ten soldiers and their officers, had been the whole of it, the guardpost would have fallen.

Stark and the Irnanese were almost at the gate when the second ten came through, a solid wedge of leather and metal. This would be the off-shift, the delay just long enough for them to turn out and get their gear on.

Weight of shield and armored bodies bore the swordsmen back. Short blades stabbed, cutting through thick furs. The first lot of Thyrans rallied, the seven or eight who could still fight. They concentrated on the tall Southrons, beating them back into the lines of the gray men.

The brothers fell, almost in the same moment. Halk went to one knee, his hand at his side where blood poured out through a rent in his tunic. Heavy boots kicked him down and trampled over him. Breca screamed like an eagle. Her long blade took the head clean from a Thyran's shoulders and then she went down beneath a wall of shields.

Stark had lost sight of Gerrith. He was among the gray warriors now, the ones who had formed a guard around the Corn King and his priests. These were pressed back against the cliff, standing quietly with folded arms. Stark, running sweat and blood, beating aside the short stabbing swords that forced him ever backward, shouted furiously to Hargoth, "Where is your magic, Corn King?"

Hargoth answered, "Where are your stars?" And his eyes shone like bitter ice through the holes of his mask.

The gray men fell, or were driven into the claws of the Outdwellers, who slashed them from behind, or pushed them over the edge into the ravine. Their slings were useless, their javelins spent or broken against the Thyran armor. Stark caught a glimpse of the twin lightning strokes being separated by a blow that split Kintoth's narrow skull to the jawbone. He felt rock against his back. The wall of shields came in against him. He struck up and under, felt the blade go home, and lost it as the man fell, taking the sword with him. The shield-wall battered him with iron bosses, drove the breath from his lungs. He snarled and clawed and bit, all humanness lost in pain and a growing dark. The Thyrans came on, as merciless as time. And at last, the darkness was all.

When light returned to him, it was the light of Old Sun, running rusty on the stones of a square courtyard enclosed by thick walls. He was inside the guardpost. He was cold and he hurt, and he had bled somewhat onto the stones where he lay. He was not dead, and he thought after a while that he was not dying. A name came into his head.

Gerrith.

A stab of fear contracted his belly. He tried to sit up, and found that his hands were bound. He wondered if a man could learn to live his whole life with his hands bound.

He did not sit up, but he achieved a wider view.

Halk leaned against the wall nearby. His eyes were shut and he breathed through his mouth, shallow careful breaths. His face had a gray pallor; it seemed to have fallen in around the bones. His tunic was open, showing a rough wad of bandage. Beyond him, Hargoth and his priests sat in a group. They appeared soiled and bruised but not wounded, and their masks had been left on them. A guard stood over them, watchful against sorceries. In another place were such of their warriors as had survived, only seven and most of them wounded. All were bound.

He did not see Gerrith.

He called her name, and she spoke from behind him.

"I'm here, Stark." He floundered about, pushing his back up against the wall, and she tried to help him. Her hands were tied. She did not seem to be hurt, except for bruises, and her hair hung loose around her face.

"Why," he asked her, "in the name of all the starry hells of space did you insist on coming?"

He was furious with her.

There was much activity in the courtyard, almost a holiday air. Thyran soldiers went about various sorts of business. Their dead and wounded were laid out on litters. A cluster of Outdwellers, like ragged crows, stood by a doorway and grabbed for bundles of provisions being handed out to them. Their payment, no doubt, for betrayal.

One of them saw that Stark was conscious. He came over and looked down with malevolent pleasure. It was the piper. Stark could see the instrument peeping out from his untidy wrappings.

"Why?" asked Stark.

"They told us to watch for you. They told us how you looked. They promised to pay us. But we would have done it for nothing."

The pupils of his eyes had contracted. They reflected nothing now but hate.

Again Stark asked, "Why?"

"The stars are sacred," said the piper. "They are the eyes of the Goddess. When our souls take flight the bright eyes see them, and the arms of the Goddess reach out to gather them in. You wish to defile the stars and rob us of all bliss."

Stark said wearily, "I don't think you understand." Normally he was tolerant of tribal fancies, but he felt no great tenderness for the Outdwellers. "The stars are already defiled. They're only suns, like that one over your head. They have worlds around them, like this one under your feet. People live on those worlds, people who never heard of Outdwellers or their footling goddess. And the starships fly between them. It's all going on out there, this second as you stand here, and nothing you can do will stop it."

The piper carried his peculiar weapons, along with his pipe. He thrust one hand in and out of his garments so swiftly that Stark could barely follow the motion. Sharp claws flashed upward, ready for the death-stroke, and Stark had just time enough to consider the wisdom of his remarks. Then a hairy fist closed on the piper's broomstick arm, and a Thyran officer with an iron torque around his neck said cheerfully, "Do you drop it, or do I break your wrist?"

The piper wriggled his fingers and let the claws go clacking onto the stones.

"This one's worth more alive," said the Thyran, and let go. He wiped his hand on his breeches. "Go along with you, filth."

The piper gathered up his armament and went. The Outdwellers began to file out through the gate, glancing back as they did so with hateful leers at the captives. Stark suddenly sat up straighter and looked again around the courtyard.

"I see your dead," he said to the Thyran. "I do not see ours."

"Don't worry, friend. The Outdwellers will give them useful burial." The Thyran examined him with interest. "You put us to some pains to keep from killing you."

"Why did you?"

"That was the order. Dead if necessary, alive if possible and double the reward. Same for the woman, and for this man. The others—" He shrugged. "Dead was good enough."

Halk's eyes had opened. "Breca was my shield-mate. The men were my comrades. You killed them. That was fair enough, since we came against you. But to give them to those vermin for—" He could not finish the sentence. Rage choked him. Incredibly, he came to his feet and was reaching for the Thyran's throat with his bound hands. His wound betrayed him and he fell again, to stare half blind at Stark with such hatred as might kill a man where he sat.

"Prophecies!" Halk said, and sobbed once, a racking sound that shook his whole body. Then he fainted.

Stark wished that he had left Halk and the others in Amnir's wagons, sleeping the sleep of the Goddess.

Hargoth and the priests were watching him, and he could not bear that gaze, either, even though he had never asked for their faith. He asked the Thyran, "Who are 'they' who gave you the orders, and what are we waiting for?"

The Thyran smiled. "As to 'they,' you'll meet them soon enough. And we're waiting for men to come up from the city, to take over the post while we go down with you and our wounded. You left us short-handed."

There was a second gate, in the wall opposite the one through which the Outdwellers had gone. A couple of soldiers were up above, keeping an eye out over whatever country lay beyond. The Thyran glanced at them, and then he laughed.

"You wanted the Outdwellers to show you a way around Thyra. There isn't any way around. We guard every trail, every approach. Not a puff of wind can get past us. Otherwise, anyone could creep in and nibble away our wealth."

He kicked Stark experimentally, studied the dried blood that showed on him, cocking his head from side to side. He stepped back, turning to Hargoth.

"I don't believe he's from the stars at all. He's just meat like the rest of us. And none too bright, either, to take up with the Gray Maggots. A fine lot altogether, to make big talk about flying up to heaven!"

His broad face beamed with the scornful smugness of absolutely sublime stupidity. Stark hated him.

"Aren't you even curious?" he asked. "A million worlds out there with more wonders than I could tell you in a million years, and you don't even want to ask a question?"

The Thyran shrugged, heaving his weight of iron bosses up and down. "Why should I care what's out there? What more could I find anywhere than I already have here in Thyra?"

He walked away. "Well," said Stark, "and there's no answer to that." He leaned back against the wall, infinitely tired. "What do you say now, wise woman?"

Hargoth gave her no chance to speak. "The only way was south. South! South where the ships are."

"The Spring Child told you otherwise."

"A false augury. A punishment. Because of your lust for that woman, you cheated Old Sun of his gift. He sent us a curse instead of a blessing."

The eight heads of the priests nodded solemnly. Nine pairs of eyes pierced him with malevolence.

"You are not the Promised One."

"I never claimed to be," said Stark. "Was it because of your anger that you didn't use your magic to help us?"

"The Goddess does not send us power like a lightning bolt. It is a slow magic. We had no time."

"You have time now."

Impatiently Hargoth said, "How can we perform the ritual? How stand as we must, and think as we must? You know little of sorcery."

Stark knew enough of it not to depend on it. He gave up the conversation.

"Have faith," said Gerrith softly.

"Faith?" said Stark. "Will it produce us another miracle that leads nowhere?"

The guards above the gate sang out. Stark heard the marching drumbeat in the distance. Presently the gate was opened and the replacements tramped in. A period of ordered chaos followed as the change-over was made. The outgoing force formed ranks. The litters were picked up. Ungently the captives were made to rise.

Halk was conscious again. He fell twice trying to get up, with a Thyran boot to help him. Stark swung his hands in a short vicious arc and knocked the soldier clanging against the wall.

"He needs a litter," said Stark, "and don't draw that blade. I'm worth double alive and your officers won't thank you for robbing them."

The sword hesitated, halfway out of the sheath. The officer with the iron torque came up.

"Put that away," he said to the soldier, and then he hit Stark backhanded across the face. "You trade overmuch on your value."

"He needs a litter," Stark said.

Halk swore that he did not and tried again to get up. He fell a third time. The officer shouted for litter-bearers.

"Now, then," he said, "move!" He shoved Stark into line.

The drummers picked up the steady beat. The company marched out through the gate.

The path on this side of the guardpost ran for a time under the flank of a ridge that shut off any view of what lay beyond. Then it swung around a curve and the prospect opened up, suddenly and with spectacular effect.

The Witchfires thrust sharply into the sky, throwing back Old Sun's sullen gleaming. At their feet, covering a portion of the foothills and spreading out across a broad valley, was the ruin of a city.

It had probably begun, Stark thought, as a strong fortress in the days when fighting men and caravans moved back and forth through the pass of the Witchfires, which was like a wide notch between the peaks. Later it had become a city, and then a metropolis, and then a dead and silent corpse, sinking in upon itself with the weight of wind and frost and endless time, until all its original form was lost and it was only a great, dark, many-humped mound beneath the mountains.

Then from somewhere the Thyrans had come, Strayer's men, the People of the Hammer; and the city had taken on a strange new life. Now, in the dim coppery glare of day, the guardian of the pass appeared more like a doorkeeper at the gate of hell. All around the base of the city, and into its ugly flanks, and among its heaped debris, were fumaroles from which came plumes of smoke and red glarings that pulsed and shook.

"The forges are never cold," said the Thyran officer. "We are all smiths, even as we are all soldiers. We work and we guard. This is how Strayer taught us."

It sounded a dull life, but Stark forebore to say so. The inside of his mouth was still bleeding.

Some two hours of marching brought them into the new city.

It lacked beauty. Some of the dwellings were underground, some partly so. Others, built of stone from the hills and debris quarried from the old city, were above ground but squat and low, with few windows to take the cold.

A vast straggle of frozen lanes ran between the dwellings. There were places for pens and livestock, and near them a band of hairy folk leading a string of animals made way for the soldiers, staring out of filthy faces at the prisoners. The animals bore great stacks of dried lichens.

There was a lot of smoke, blowing constantly, and a muffled sound of hammering that went on like heartbeats. Huge piles of rusty scrap metal bulked here and there, and over all was the old city, a tangled mountain blotting out part of the Witchfires. Over the centuries the Thyrans had chewed and tunneled the mountain ragged round its edges, and dug dwellings into this raggedness like caves, opening dark mouths into the deeper bowels of the ruin. Stark thought of a community of rats living in the biggest junkyard in the world. If the Thyrans were able to reclaim even a small fraction of the countless tons of metal buried in that junkyard, they could keep themselves busy for another thousand years.

The company swung into what was evidently the

street that led up from the main gate. It was much wider than the lanes, and it ran almost straight.

The thudding of the drums became sharper, the pace of the men smartened. People were swarming out to see them go by. They were chiefly of the same heavy build, though occasionally there were individuals of a different shape and coloring to attest to outside blood. The women were no more prepossessing than the men. Stark had no idea what the women of the Towers looked like, but they could only have been an improvement. These people shouted to the soldiers, crowding in to stare and push at the captives. The fur-clad children yelled insults and threw things.

The soldiers shoved the people back with bone-breaking good nature. The crisp beat of the drums never faltered. The company marched up the straight street, straight to the Iron House.

The dark walls of the Iron House were burnished like a shield. The metal sheathing of the roof shone with a dull luster in the light of the ginger star. A guard of twelve men was drawn up before massive iron doors that bore the hammer device. The House was rectangular, some eighty feet long by half that many wide, the long way oriented north and south. The doors were in the southern front. At the northern end, close against the ruins, were lower wings of stone and rubble.

The drums sounded a long roll. The heavy doors swung open. The company marched into a great hall.

Fires burned in pits, giving out heat and smoke. At the far end of the hall was a dais, with a high seat and several places of honor. The high seat was made of iron, strong, square, without grace or ornamentation. A man wearing an iron collar and pectoral sat in it; he was also strong and square and without grace. The pectoral on his barrel chest was in the form of a hammer.

There were others on the dais, in the seats of honor, and Stark saw with no surprise at all that the man on the right of the high seat was Gelmar of Skeg.

20

People came into the hall behind the soldiers. The chief men beat and shouldered their way through the press to crowd up onto the dais or take their places below it, according to rank. Lesser men filled the body of the hall. Women remained outside, and small boys who darted in were pitched out bodily. The iron doors clanged shut. As though that were a signal, the men began shouting, "Strayer! Strayer and the forges!" They stamped their feet and slapped their weapons. "Strayer!"

After that ritual shout the hall settled gradually to a breathy silence, undertoned with rustlings and coughings. The smoky air became charged with a smell of heat and sweat, wool and fur and leather.

A clear space had been left around the soldiers. The officer drew his sword and lifted the hilt in salute.

"These are the captives, Ironmaster."

The Ironmaster wore a fine purple robe. The cloth must have come up from the south in Amnir's wagons; the local weave was coarse and undyed. He nodded his grizzled head and the officer put away his sword.

The Ironmaster turned to Gelmar. "Are these the ones you wanted?"

Gelmar rose and came down from the dais. He wore a tunic of the somber red Stark remembered from Skeg, and he carried his wand of office. He came without haste, and he looked at Stark with cool deliberation. On the dais were three other Wandsmen, wearing green. One of them, in a seat next to Gelmar's, had a face deep-scarred and half blinded by a sword cut that had left an ugly groove from forehead to jaw. The wound was healed, but still showed an angry color. This man leaned forward in his chair, with the hunched quiver of an animal about to spring.

Gelmar looked into Stark's eyes, and his own were dark and somehow veiled, lacking the fire of triumph Stark had expected. Yet there was a cold ferocity about them that was frightening.

"I know this man," said Gelmar. "Yes. Concerning the others—" He beckoned to the scarred man on the dais. "Vasth?"

Vasth came quickly to peer into Gerrith's face.

"There were two women," said the Thyran officer. "One of them fought like a man. A shield-bearer, as we had been told. These Southrons defy all morality, allowing women to handle swords. We were forced to kill her."

"No matter," said Vasth. "This woman is Gerrith, the daughter of Gerrith. And this—" He turned to Halk on his litter. "This one is Halk, a ringleader, a killer of Wandsmen. I have cause to remember him." He traced the groove of the scar. "He gave me this."

"A pity my hand was weak in that moment," said Halk. He had not stood the journey well. He looked past the green Wandsman to Gelmar. "What has happened to Irnan?"

"Irnan has fallen," said Gelmar, and his mouth was cruel. "So much for all your trouble."

"And Ashton?" asked Stark.

"Ashton," said Gelmar, and smiled, a small twisting of the lips as one might twist a knife blade in the yielding flesh. "The Lords Protector were discussing what should be done with him when I left the Citadel. That decision will have been made by now. Perhaps he lives, perhaps he is already dead. I can't tell you. But you'll know soon enough." He turned from Stark to face the Corn King and his priests.

Stark made one violent movement and was instantly quelled.

Gelmar took no notice of him. "You were with these rebels, Hargoth, coming to attack us at the Citadel. Why did you do this folly?"

"Because we want the freedom of the stars."

Hargoth still had his pride. His narrow head was as erect as ever, his eyes met Gelmar's defiantly. "The man Stark and the Sun Woman told us that you, the Wandsmen, forbade this and so we must destroy you. We believed an omen; we believed them. But they were false prophets. They would not go south where the ships are. They cheated Old Sun, because of the lust of their bodies. And because we believed them, we have been punished."

Gelmar nodded. He said, "The ships are gone from the south, Hargoth. Do you understand that?"

"I understand."

"The ships are gone. The foreign men and their ways are gone with them. The star-roads are closed. Our way lies as it always has, with Skaith and Old Sun. Do you understand that?"

Hargoth said, "I understand." In his voice was the deadness of understanding.

"Then go and tell your people, Hargoth."

Hargoth bent his head.

Gelmar spoke to the dais, to the man in purple who watched smiling, pleased by the humbling of the gray men of the Towers.

"Open your doors, Ironmaster. Let them go."

"I had rather see them slain," said the Ironmaster. "But—" He shrugged and ordered the doors to be opened.

The priests and warriors formed their meager ranks, beaten men, acquiescing not with patience but with anger.

And Hargoth said, "Wait."

He faced Gerrith. "You prophesied for me, Sun Woman. Now I prophesy for you. Your body will yet feed Old Sun, though not as a parting gift."

Gerrith's expression had changed. All the way from the guardpost she had looked tired to exhaustion, merely enduring. Now she seemed to be listening intently to some inner voice. Yet she heard Hargoth and answered him.

"That may be. But your people must find themselves a new Corn King, for you lead them badly. You cast the finger-bones and you prophesy, but you do not know truth from falsehood."

Her head came erect, and her voice rang out strongly.

"Irnan has not fallen. The ships have not gone from Skaith. The star-roads are open. New things are here, and the Wandsmen are afraid. In the end—"

Vasth struck her, viciously. Blood sprang from her mouth and she fell, past Stark with his bound hands, into the arms of a Thyran soldier, who caught her awkwardly.

"We have had enough of wise women," said Vasth.

The hall had become suddenly still. In that stillness Gelmar spoke softly to Hargoth.

"Will you go?"

Hargoth turned and went, his priests and the remnant of his warriors following after.

Gelmar clapped his hands.

Men came in through a leather-curtained doorway at the side of the hall. They wore saffron-colored tunics and richly ornamented collars of some bright metal. They were of a breed that Stark had not seen before, one of the many things on Skaith he had not seen—beautiful men, beautifully proportioned, with aquiline faces almost too perfect, and they were so much alike that it was difficult to tell one from another, except for the color of the hair. This ranged from black to a reddish blond, but all had copper-colored eyes. The eyes were too wide apart and too long for their faces, and there was something odd about them. As they came closer, Stark saw what it was. They were like the inlaid eyes of statues, startlingly lifelike but without life, showing brilliance but no depth.

As though they understood without orders what they must do, two of them picked up Halk's litter, and another helped Gerrith to her feet. Two more replaced the Thyran soldiers beside Stark. They had daggers at their belts, and smooth muscles showed powerfully beneath their tunics. A sixth man stood by, and it was to him that Gelmar spoke.

"Take them now. Guard them."

Stark saw Gelmar's face clearly, very clearly. The lines, the tautness, the weariness. Some of that proud high confidence that he remembered from their first meeting had been left forever in the sea where Stark had taken him.

Stark said, "Gerrith is right. You are afraid."

Gelmar's men had them moving almost before the words were said, and Gelmar ignored him. No one beyond their small group had even heard him. But Stark knew that what he said was true.

New things had come, things the Wandsmen could neither control nor comprehend, and they felt their ancient power threatening to slip away from them. They must grasp it now and hold it firmly, regardless of the cost, or else it would be gone.

And grasp it they would, with all their strength, in whatever way seemed best to them. The fear, and the uncertainty, would only make them more dangerous.

And might already have cost Ashton his life.

The captives were taken into one of the adjoining wings, to a room rudely furnished with sleeping mats and a few random articles. The Thyrans seemed not to indulge themselves in luxury but the mats at least offered some comfort.

The men in the saffron tunics stayed, all six of them, to guard a woman and two men, and one of those wounded. It was a measure of their importance.

Gerrith was making a dazed and fumbling attempt to wipe some of the blood from her face. Halk said,

"Gerrith, what you said about Irnan—was it true?"

Answering for her, Stark said harshly, "Of course it's true. Why else would they want us alive? If the revolt were really over, dead would be good enough."

In a curiously gentle voice, one of the bright-eyed men said, "Do not talk."

Halk ignored him. He seemed to have recovered a measure of strength, even of eagerness. "Yes, I see. If Irnan still stands, then perhaps other city-states have joined her—"

He broke off with a gasp of pain as the man nearest him kicked the frame of the litter.

If that were so, thought Stark, it would not be enough for the Wandsmen to announce that the wise woman and the Dark Man and the ringleaders of the revolt were all dead and the prophecy come to nothing. They would have to produce real evidence, and parade it before people who knew and could attest to its authenticity. Gerrith alive, the Dark Man alive, one undoubted ringleader alive—all captives of the Wandsmen, proof that the prophecy was a lie and the power of the Lords Protector invincible. Gelmar and his aides could keep the three of them in cages for the rest of their lives, dragging them up and down the roads of Skaith. Or a fitting end could be devised for them, a very public end, with recantings and repentance—an end to remain vivid for generations in the minds of the people.

Then, if hope of the fulfillment of the prophecy had anything to do with keeping the revolt alive, it would collapse very quickly. Irnan would fall, and that would be the end of it. For the present, at least.

The Wandsmen obviously believed that that hope was keeping the revolt alive. Stark believed it too. Not because the Irnanese were childishly superstitious, but because if the Citadel and the Lords Protector were not destroyed, they could not hold out alone against the mobs of Farers and whatever mercenary troops the Wandsmen would send against them. Their allies, present or potential, among the other city-states then would fall away. Jerann himself had said that these others would wait and see what happened.

The Citadel and the Lords Protector. It all came back to them. They were the symbol of permanence—the unchanging, the holy and unseen and forever inviolate power.

The power that would by now have pronounced judgment on Ashton.

Was it, after all, a power that a man could fight? Even if he were free?

Stark looked at his bound wrists. The thongs were wet with his blood. The six men crowded the small room, watching. They had orders not to kill him, he didn't doubt. But there are worse things to do to a man than killing him.

Six men between him and the door. Beyond the door, the Iron House, and beyond that, Thyra. With every gate and every path guarded. Not a puff of wind could get through.

Halk had had second thoughts. "Why would Gelmar lie to Hargoth?"

Again the litter was kicked.

Again Stark answered, speaking rapidly, eye on the nearest guard.

"Does he want the People of the Towers marching south . . ."

He dodged the first blow, stiffened fingers aimed at his throat.

". . . singing the Hymn of Deliverance?"

The second blow he could not dodge. He didn't try. He caught the vicious fingers between his teeth.

He learned one thing. These too-perfect creatures were not automatons. They bled.

So did he.

After a time a healer came, a Thyran in a tunic both

undyed and unwashed. He wore a chain of office around his neck and was followed by two boys bearing pots of ointment and bundles of rags. The healer tended their hurts, spending long minutes over Halk, grumbling at wasting his time and talents on a non-Thyran who would probably die anyway. When he was finished, servants came and fed them, and then they were told to rest in preparation for a journey. Gelmar seemed to be in great haste.

The room was stiflingly close. The powerful bodies of the men in the saffron tunics were oppressive in the confined space. The smell of them was repulsive to Stark. They smelled like snakes. Nevertheless, he managed to sleep until men came in with new manacles for them, fresh from Strayer's forges. Gelmar's man with the bitten hand held his sword-point at Stark's groin while the irons were fastened on; his face had still shown no expression, not even pain.

Gerrith seemed to have awakened from a dream, and not a pleasant one. She was careful not to look at Stark.

When the Lamp of the North was above the peaks, they were taken out of the room and marched along a corridor to a yard beside the Iron House, where men and beasts were waiting. The beasts were small, with shaggy hair that swept the ground and sharp horns tipped with metal balls to prevent them hooking. The men who led them wore bulky garments of skins with the fur inside, and only their eyes showed between heavy caps and thick tangled beards. The beards were flocked with white as though the snow had got into them; it did not seem to be a sign of age. Stark guessed that these were Harsenyi, in the service of the Wandsmen.

For a moment the prisoners were close together, and Gerrith managed to touch Stark's hand and smile at him. A strange smile.

It was as though she had said goodbye.

21

The beasts shuffled and blew, breath puffing white in the icy air. Stark and Gerrith were made to mount, with a guard on either side, afoot. Halk was transferred to a traveling litter slung between two of the animals. He appeared to be unconscious or asleep most of the time. Even so, he had been manacled like the others, and a guard stood at the head of his litter.

Gelmar, cloaked and hooded for the journey, came and bent over him, feeling Halk's throat where the life beat in it.

"Cover him well," he said to the beautiful man by the litter. "If he reaches the Citadel alive, we can heal him."

The beautiful man, with sword and dagger belted now over a rich outer tunic, covered Halk carefully with furs.

Gelmar and the lesser Wandsmen mounted. The retainers, twelve in all, portioned themselves out along the line, walking near the Harsenyi but obviously disdainful of them.

An escort of Thyran troops tramped up, banging the inevitable drum. The cavalcade started.

They passed through the gate and turned north toward the night-sparkle of the Witchfires. The escort saw them past the outer guardpost, then saluted and went drumming and clanking back to the city.

The path lay ahead, climbing a long gradient to the summit. Somewhere on the other side of the mountains was the Citadel. In a way, Stark thought, getting there was going to be easier than he had thought. At least he would not have to worry about the Northhounds.

No wagons had come this way in centuries, and the

track was narrow. The hard little hoofs of the beasts clattered steadily on the frozen ground. The sky was a glory of shifting color.

It was bright enough to see quite clearly the shapes that thronged the pass.

For geological ages the forces of wind and water, thaw and freeze, had worked at the rock walls, scouring, carving, polishing, wearing away. Sheathed in ice, the sculptures seemed alive in the shaking light of the aurora. Great faces watched with deep-gouged eyes. Towering pinnacles soared and tottered, gargoyle wings spread out to shadow the little humans passing beneath. In the wider places, where softer strata had been carried off, whole crowds of cowled and hooded forms seemed to whisper together. The wind from the high north blew down the pass, chuckling and singing, talking to the shining creatures it had helped to create.

Stark's human reason told him that these monsters were no more than lumps of eroded stone. His mind knew that. His primitive gut said otherwise. And his animal senses told him that other beings not of stone were close by.

The Children of Skaith-Our-Mother?

He could not see anything, but a regiment might have hidden itself in the eccentricities of the rock. Still, the Wandsmen and their retainers, even the beasts, moved on confidently. If there was something here, they were accustomed to it and not afraid.

The manacles weighed heavily on Stark's wrists. The sky flared. White, pure as the veils of angels. Pale green, delicate as shoal-water. Red, like a fire of roses. From time to time the shimmering curtains drew apart to show the velvet darkness beyond, with the green star glowing.

Gerrith rode ahead of him, sitting her little beast quietly, her head bowed as though she rode toward an ordeal. He wished he knew what she had dreamed.

At length, just below the summit, at the right-hand side of the pass, he saw a tall pinnacle standing, canted forward until it seemed that it must fall of its own weight. It had the form of an elongated man in an attitude of prayer, and about its base irregular groups and lines of hooded figures stood as though they listened.

In the shifting light and shadow of the aurora, three of the figures moved, detached themselves from the stone, came into the center of the pass and stood barring the way.

And now the little beasts snorted and danced. The cavalcade came to a halt beneath the leaning man.

Gelmar rode forward. "Kell à Marg," he said. "Skaith-Daughter." His voice had a flat quality, as though he were holding it in rigid check. "Fenn. Ferdic."

The figures were cloaked against the wind but their heads were bare except for diadems of wrought gold. The diadem of the foremost figure was set with a great smoky jewel. There was something peculiar about the three faces, very pale in the aurora-light.

Kell à Marg said, "Gelmar." The voice was like chiming bells. It was a woman's voice, imperious in spite of its music, with the innate arrogance of unquestioned power. A match for Gelmar, Stark thought. He had made out the peculiarity of the faces. They were covered in fine white fur, and the features, while not unpleasing, were distorted subtly from the human—the noses blunted, the jaws prominent. The woman had eyes as huge and dark and glowing as the jewel she wore. Night-creature's eyes. She said to Gelmar,

"Did you think to pass through our mountains without pause?"

"Skaith-Daughter," said Gelmar, and now there was just the faintest edge of irritation in his voice, "we have an urgent mission and time is short. I thank you for this honor, but—"

"No honor," said Kell à Marg. She looked past him at the captives. "These are the wicked ones you were seeking?"

"Kell à Marg—"

"You've been setting the whole of the north by its ears; it's small wonder we know. Even in our deep caverns, we're not deaf."

The edge of irritation had sharpened. "Kell à Marg, I told you—"

"You told me there was a threat to Skaith, something new and strange that only you of the Citadel could deal with. You told me only because I asked you—because the Harsenyi had brought us tales we could not understand."

"There was no need to concern yourself."

"You take too much on your shoulders, Gelmar. You intend to settle the entire future of Skaith-Our-Mother without consulting us, her Children."

"There is no time, Kell à Marg! I must take these people south as soon as possible."

"You will make time," said Kell à Marg.

There was a silence. The wind from the high north whined and chuckled. The hooded figures listened dutifully to the endless prayer of the leaning man. The cloaks of the Children fluttered.

Gelmar said, "I beg you not to interfere." Irritation had become desperation. He knew this woman, Stark thought. Knew her and feared her, disliked her intensely. "I understand these people, I've dealt with them, I know what must be done. Please, let us pass."

The ground shook, ever so slightly. Above their heads the leaning man seemed to sway.

"Kell à Marg!"

"Yes, Wandsman?"

A second small quivering. Pebbles rattled down. The leaning man bowed. The Harsenyi began hastily to move themselves and their beasts out from under those tons of rock.

"Very well!" said Gelmar furiously. "I will make time."

Kell à Marg said briskly, "The Harsenyi may enter and wait in the usual place."

She turned and walked with a lithe, undulant stride toward the cliff. There was a sort of lane between the stone figures. She went along it, with Fenn and Ferdic, and the cavalcade followed meekly. Gelmar's stiff back was eloquent of stifled rage.

Gerrith had straightened up. Her head was high. High and proud. Stark felt a qualm of alarm not connected with the Children or the threatening quality of the cliff which, he knew, was about to swallow them. They had already alarmed him, but this was different. He wondered again what she knew, and damned all prophetic visions for the thousandth time.

Halk's voice came from the litter, weak but still jeering. "I told you you could not escape the Children by talking them away."

A great slab of stone opened in the cliff face, moving easily on its pivots. The cavalcade passed through.

The door swung shut. Kell à Marg flung back her cloak. "I do so hate the wind!" she said, and looked at Gelmar, smiling.

They were in a large cavern, evidently the place where the Harsenyi customarily came to trade with the Children. Lamps burned dimly in the quiet air, giving off a scent of sweet oil. The walls were rough, the floor uneven. At its inner side there was a second door.

"The lesser Wandsmen are not needed," said Kell à Marg. "I think we'll get little good from the wounded man, so he may stay here as well. Those two—" She pointed to Stark and Gerrith. "The wise woman and the one called, I believe, the Dark Man. I want them. And of course, Gelmar, I require your counsel."

The green Wandsmen accepted their dismissal with bad grace; Vasth looked poisonous but held his tongue. Gelmar's jaw was tightly set. He could barely control his anger.

"I shall need guards," he said, cutting the words very short. "This man Stark is dangerous."

"Even in irons?"

"Even in irons."

"Four of your creatures, then. Though I fail to see how he could hope to escape from the House of the Mother."

There was a shuffle of dismounting. Kell à Marg stood easily, waiting with her courtiers. Stark knew without being told that she did not often stand this way, in this outer cavern, with the nomads. This was a special occasion, one of sufficient urgency to make her break precedent. She was looking at him with frank curiosity.

He looked at her. The cloak tossed back over slender shoulders revealed a lean body as arrogant as her voice, clad in its own sleek white fur and ornamented with a light harness of the same wrought gold as the diadem. A beautiful animal, a voluptuous woman. A great royal ermine with wicked eyes. Stark felt no stirring of excitement.

She lifted a shoulder daintily. "This one may or may not be as dangerous as you say, but it's bold enough." She turned and led the way to the inner door. It swung silently open.

Kell à Marg strode through it. Gelmar, his two captives, and his guards followed after, with the wiry white-furred courtiers bringing up the rear.

Attendants who had opened the door swung it shut again behind them, and they were closed into a strange and beautiful world.

Stark shivered, a shallow animal rippling of the skin.

The House of the Mother smelled of sweet oil, of dust and depth and caverns.

It smelled of death.

22

They were in a corridor, wide and high, lighted by the flickering lamps. A group of people were waiting there. They bent their heads with the pale fur and the close-set ears and the golden diadems that varied in size and splendor according to rank. A murmur of voices repeated reverently, "Skaith-Daughter. You have returned."

Stark thought they had been waiting a long time and were tired of standing. At one side he noticed four of the Children gathered together, apart from the others. They bore themselves with a separate pride. They were clad in skull-caps and tabards of some black material, close-belted with golden chains, and they did not bow. Their collective gaze went immediately to the strangers.

Courtiers and officials, when they straightened up, also fixed Stark and Gerrith with cold and hostile eyes. Wandsmen they were apparently used to, for they spared Gelmar only an unwelcoming glance. The strangers seemed to disturb them deeply.

"I will speak with the Diviners," said Kell à Marg, and gestured the courtiers out of the way.

The black-clad ones fell in around Kell à Marg. They five walked ahead, speaking in low voices. The courtiers and officials had to be content with the last place in line.

They walked for what seemed a long while. The walls and roof of the corridor were covered with carvings, some in high relief, others almost in the round. They were done with great artistry. They appeared to have something to do with the history or the religion of the Children. Some of the history, Stark judged, might have been stormy. There were places where the carvings had been damaged and repaired, and he counted six doors in the first stretch that could be closed against invaders.

Chambers opened off the corridor. They had magnificently carved doorways, and what he could see of their interiors gave an astonishing impression of richness. Pierced lamps of silver picked out gleams of color, of inlay and mosiac, touched the *outré* shapes of things that Stark could only guess at. One thing was certain; these Children of Skaith-Our-Mother had little in common with their cousins of the Sea. Far from being animals, they had what was obviously a complex and highly developed society, working away here beneath the glittering peaks of the Witchfires.

Or ought he to say "had once had?"

Some of the chambers were unlighted. Others had only one or two lamps in their large darkness. There was that subtle odor of dust and death, a feeling that the comings and goings glimpsed in the branching corridors and the work, whatever it might be, that was going on, were all less than they should be in the House of the Mother.

The corridor ended in an enormous cavern, a natural one where the fantastic rock formations had been left untouched. There were lamps enough here, and a royal path of marble blocks set into the floor. Beyond was a series of jewel-box ante-rooms, and then the vaulted chamber that must belong to Kell à Marg, Skaith-Daughter.

It was perfectly plain. Walls and floor were faced with some luminous white stone, without carving or ornamentation. It was completely bare. Nothing was allowed to distract the eye from the focal point of the room, the high seat.

Kell à Marg climbed the broad steps to the dais and sat herself.

The high seat was carved from rich brown rock the color of loam, and the shape of it was a robed woman, seated to hold Skaith-Daughter on her knees, her arms curved round protectively, her head bent forward in an attitude of affection. Kell à Marg sat with her hands on the hands of Skaith-Mother, and her slim, arrogant body gleamed against the dark stone.

The Diviners stood in a little group at her right, the others were scattered around the spacious emptiness, close to the high seat; Fenn and Ferdic were at her left. Gelmar, Stark, Gerrith, and the guards were together at the foot of the steps.

"Now," said Kell à Marg, "tell me again of this danger that has come to Skaith."

Gelmar had taken firm hold of himself. His voice was almost pleasant.

"Certainly, Skaith-Daughter. But I would prefer to do it more privately."

"These about me are the Keepers of the House, Gelmar. The Clan Mothers, the men and women who are responsible for the well-being of my people. I wish them to hear."

Gelmar nodded. He looked at Stark and Gerrith. "Only let these two be taken out."

"Ah," said Kell à Marg. "The captives. No, Gelmar. They stay."

Gelmar began an angry protest, smothered it, inclined his head, and began to tell the story of the ships.

Kell à Marg listened attentively. So did Fenn and Ferdic, the Clan Mothers and the counselors. Under the attentiveness was fear, and something else. Anger, hate —the instinctive rejection of an intolerable truth.

"Let me be clear about what you say," said Kell à Marg. "These ships. They come from outside, from far away?"

"From the stars."

"The stars. We had almost forgotten them. And the men who fly in these ships, they also come from outside? They are not born of Skaith-Mother?"

The glowing eyes of the Clan Mothers and the counselors looked at Stark, looked at blasphemy.

"That is so," said Gelmar. "They are alien to us, completely. We let them stay because they brought us things we lack, such as metals. But they brought us worse—off-world ways, foreign ideas. And they corrupted some of our people."

"They corrupted us with hope," said Gerrith. "Skaith-Daughter, let me tell you how we live under the rule of the Lords Protector and their Wandsmen."

Gelmar would have liked to stop her, but Kell à Marg silenced him. She listened while Gerrith spoke. When she had finished, Kell à Marg said,

"You and your people wished to get into these ships and fly to another world, away from Skaith? You wished to live on alien soil, which never gave you breath?"

"Yes, Skaith-Daughter. It may be difficult for you to understand. We looked upon it as salvation."

It was the wrong thing to say. She knew it. Stark knew it. Yet it had to be said.

"We found a different salvation," said Kell à Marg. "We returned to the womb of the Mother, and while your people starved and clawed and died under Old Sun, we lived warm and fed and comfortable, secure in the Mother's love. Do not expect me to weep for you, nor to care about what the Wandsmen do in their own place. I have a larger concern than that."

She turned to Gelmar. "This revolt still goes on."

Reluctantly, he said, "It does."

"Well," said Stark, "and we knew that."

Kell à Marg continued. "You intend to take these people south. Why?"

"There was a prophecy—"

"Yes," said Kell à Marg. "The Harsenyi brought us some gossip about that. It concerned this man, did it not?" She looked at Stark.

Gelmar appeared anxious to hurry by this point. "It sparked the revolt. If I prove to them that the prophecy was false—"

Kell à Marg interrupted him, speaking to Gerrith. "Was this your prophecy, wise woman?"

"My mother's."

"And what did it say about this man?"

"That he would come from the stars," said Gerrith, "to destroy the Lords Protector."

Kell à Marg laughed, silvery spiteful laughter that touched Gelmar's cheekbones with a dull flush.

"I can see your concern, Gelmar! Too bad if he destroyed them before you had your turn."

"Skaith-Daughter!"

"But surely they know?" She turned to the strangers, wicked eyes alight. "Surely you know by now? The Lords Protector are only Wandsmen grown older."

Stark's heart gave a great leap. "They're human?"

"As Gelmar. That's the great reason they must remain invisible, here in the hidden north, behind their mists and their myths and their demon Northhounds. Invisibility is a condition of godhead. If folk could see them, they would know the truth, and the Lords Protector would cease to be divine. Or immortal. They would be only Wandsmen, clever enough and ambitious enough to put on white robes and spend their declining years at the Citadel wrapped in all the rewards that faithful service to their God of Goodness can bring. And these rewards are many."

Stark laughed. "Human," he said, and looked at Gelmar.

Gelmar's expression was venomous. "You need not mock, Skaith-Daughter. We serve the needy, which is more than the Children do, who serve only themselves. In the time of the Great Wandering you were asked repeatedly to give sanctuary here in the House of the Mother to folk who were dying for the lack of it, and you turned them all away."

"And so we have survived," said Kell à Marg. "Tell me, how many sufferers were taken past the Northhounds into the Citadel, to save their precious lives?"

"The Citadel is sacred . . ."

"So is the House of the Mother. The Children were here before the Citadel was built . . . "

"That is only your tradition."

". . . and we intend to be here still when it is gone. Let us return to the subject in hand. Surely a simple way exists to end your revolution. Send the ships away."

Gelmar said between his teeth, "Give me credit for some wisdom, Skaith-Daughter. Sending the ships away would solve nothing, because—"

"Because," said Stark, overriding him, "he could not make them stay away. Isn't that so, Gelmar? Isn't that why, as the wise woman said, the ships are still there, in the south?"

Again Kell à Marg held up her hand to silence Gelmar. Her hand was slender, with curving nails. There were no rings on it. The palm was pink and naked. The hand beckoned Stark to come closer, up the steps. The guards came with him.

"You are truly from another world?"

"Yes, Skaith-Daughter."

She reached out and touched his cheek. Her whole body seemed to recoil from that touch. She shivered and said, "Tell me why Gelmar could not keep the ships away."

"He has not the power. The ships come into Skeg because that is where the first ones landed, that is where the port is and the foreign enclave and the market where trading is done. It's easier and more convenient. And the Wandsmen have the appearance of control there. At least they can see what's going on."

She seemed to understand. She nodded, and said sharply to Gelmar, "Let him speak."

"If Skeg is closed to the ships, there is nothing to prevent them going anywhere else the captains think they might pick up a profit. Most ships, the smaller ones, can land where they will. The Wandsmen couldn't keep track of them; they couldn't have their mob of Farers everywhere."

"They might land even here?"

"Not in the mountains, Skaith-Daughter. But close enough."

"And they would do this for profit. For money."

"You know about those things."

"We are students of the past," she said. "Historians. We know. It is only one of the things we left behind us, that need for money."

"It's still a powerful need among men, no matter where they come from. And I think what Gelmar fears the most is that some of these ships might begin taking away people who want to leave Skaith and are willing to pay for it."

Stark was watching Gelmar's face. It was closed now, closed tight, and he thought that his guess was close to the truth.

"These ships couldn't evacuate whole populations, as the Galactic Union could, but it would be a start. Gelmar's got his fist in the dam and he's trying to hold it there, hoping that the first little drop never gets through. That's why he's so desperate to put down the revolt at Irnan before it becomes a movement. If the whole south falls into civil war, it will be the off-worlders who gain, not the Wandsmen."

Or the Lords Protector, who were only Wandsmen grown older. An unbroken chain since the first founders, renewing themselves with each generation. In that sense, they were eternal and unchanging, just as Baya had said. As eternal and unchanging as the human race.

And as vulnerable.

The room was like the inside of a great pearl, glowing softly white. Kell à Marg sat at the center of it, on the brown knees of Skaith-Mother, between the encircling arms. Her eyes were on Stark, huge and sweating and uncouth in his chains and his heavy furs, the man not born of Skaith-Mother.

He said brutally, "The thing is done, Kell à Marg. Your world has been discovered; it cannot be undiscovered. New things are here and will not go away. The Wandsmen will lose the battle in the end. Why should you help them to fight it?"

Kell à Marg turned to her diviners. "Let us ask help from the Mother."

23

The Hall of the Diviners lay at the end of a long corridor in a section of the Mother's House given over to their exclusive use. The chambers Stark could see as they passed were austere and dim, occupied by students and acolytes and lesser Diviners. The chambers had been designed for much larger numbers. Branching corridors led only to silence.

The Hall itself was round, with a vaulted roof from which a single great lamp hung, gleaming silver, intricately pierced. Beneath the lamp was a circular object, waist-high and about three feet across, covered with a finely-worked cloth. The walls, instead of being carved or faced, were covered by tapestries, apparently of a great age and holiness. A benign and gigantic woman's face looked out of them, many times repeated, made wraithlike by the fading of time but disturbing none the less, with eyes that seemed to follow every move of the people in the Hall. The great lamp was not lighted. Smaller ones on pedestals burned feebly around the circumference of the room.

No one spoke.

Acolytes entered. Reverently they lighted the silver lamp and removed the worked cloth from the object beneath it, chanting all the while.

"The Eye of the Mother," murmured the Diviners, "sees only truth."

The Eye of the Mother was a crystal, enormous, set in a massive golden frame. It was clear and lucid as a raindrop, and the light from the lamp went sparkling down into it. The Diviners ranged themselves beside it, heads bowed.

There was no high seat here. Even Kell à Marg stood. Fenn and Ferdic stood behind her. Gelmar, Stark and Gerrith, and the four guards formed a separate group, close inside the door.

Kell à Marg spoke, and the hatred in her voice was distributed about equally among the outsiders.

"You are all strangers in this House. I trust one no more than another, and all of you speak of things I do not understand and cannot judge, since they are not within my experience."

"Why would I lie, Skaith-Daughter?" Gelmar asked.

"When did the Wandsman ever live who would not lie if it suited him?" Her gaze went to Gerrith, then settled on Stark. "Gelmar I know. The woman does not pretend to be other than Skaith-born, nor does she pretend that she has seen these ships. The man does so pretend. Search his mind for me, Diviners."

The imperious hand gestured to Fenn and Ferdic, who approached Stark. The two guards who flanked him did not move. Ferdic glanced at Gelmar, who snapped something to the guards. They moved aside, but they followed as Stark was led to stand beside the crystal.

"Look," said the Diviners, "into the Eye of the Mother."

Light from the pierced lamp came and went within those lucid depths, now shallow, now deep, ever shifting, drawing the gaze down and down. "The crystal is like water, let the mind float upon it, let the mind float free . . ."

Stark smiled and shook his head. "I can't be caught that easily."

The Diviners stared at him, startled, angry.

"Do you want my memories, the things that cannot lie?" he asked them. "You may have them, freely."

Every world had its methods. He had seen too many of them and mastered too few, but he knew a little. Telepathy and mind-touch he had encountered often and was not afraid of them. The important thing was never to lose control.

He shared his memories with them, the ones that were impersonal enough for sharing.

They stood with their heads bent, but they were only pretending to look into the crystal now. That was for later on. Now they were absorbed, listening to what his mind had to tell them. The truth, for Kell à Marg. Remembering.

Remembering, briefly, the worlds of his youth and Sol, his parent star, a warmth of brilliant gold.

Remembering space, as it had first burst upon him through the simulators in the passenger quarters of a starship outbound for Altair. The stunning magnificence of myriad suns ablaze in the black sea of infinity where they swam forever on their appointed ways. The clusters, like cosmic hives of burning bees. Bright nebulae sprawled across the parsecs, piled clouds of glorious fire. Dark nebulae, where the drowned suns glimmered pale as candles. The island galaxies, unthinkably distant. The deep, wide universe with no rock roof to close it in.

Remembering finally that incredible world-city, Pax, and her incredible moon, symbols of the power of the Union.

The Diviners cried out, between agony and terror. "He has seen! He has seen, Skaith-Daughter! The night-black gulfs and the burning suns, the skies of foreign worlds." They looked at Stark as though he were a demon.

Kell à Marg nodded, very slightly. "So much we are sure of, then. Now I wish to know why this man came here."

"To search for a friend, Skaith-Daughter. Someone he loved. The Wandsmen took him, the Wandsmen may have killed him. He has a great hatred for the Wandsmen and the Lords Protector."

"I see. And the prophecy. Where is the truth of that?"

"He does not know."

"The prophecy," said Stark, "and all the trappings of a fated man were put upon me through no will of my own."

"Yet they were put upon you. Why you alone, of all the strangers?"

"I don't know. But I mean you no harm, Skaith-Daughter. Neither does Gerrith. The Wandsmen are a danger to you and the whole planet, because they don't understand at all what they're dealing with."

Gelmar said, "He lies. There is no danger to you, if you will only let us go!"

Kell à Marg stood for a long time, silent, brooding, the great royal ermine pondering over its prey. At last she said,

"You mistake me, Gelmar. I am not afraid. I am not interested in your Southrons and their revolt. I care nothing for your assurances. This man is part of a new force in the world. He may, or he may not, be important to the future of the Children, and that is all I care about. When I know, then I shall decide who goes and who does not."

She turned to the Diviners. "What does the Eye of the Mother see?"

Now they looked in earnest, deep into the heart of the crystal.

The hall became silent, so still that Stark could hear every breath that was drawn. A great uneasiness took him. This mad she-thing had complete power here, and that was not a pleasant thought.

The many faces of Skaith-Mother watched dimly from around the walls. They did not comfort him.

The waiting became intolerable. No one moved. The Diviners might have been carved from wood. The weight of the mountain pressed down on Stark. He was hot, and the manacles were heavy, broad iron cuffs with a length of chain between. He turned his head, but he

could not see Gerrith, who was still behind him somewhere, near the door.

One of the Diviners drew in a sudden breath and let it
out again. Something was happening to the Eye of the
Mother.

Stark thought at first that it was the lamp. But that
glowed as brightly as ever, and yet the light was draining
out of the great crystal, the luster dimming, dulling, dar-
kening, going from pellucid clarity to an ugly curdled
red. And Stark remembered another time, another cave,
and Gerrith's Water of Vision.

"Blood," said the Diviners to Kell à Marg. "Much
blood will be spilled if this man lives. Death will come
to the House of the Mother."

"Then," said Kell à Marg quietly, "he must die."

Stark began gathering the chain into his hands, carefully, so that it might not clink.

Gelmar stepped forward. "And he shall die. I shall
see to it myself, Skaith-Daughter."

"I shall see to it," said Kell à Marg. "Fenn! Ferdic!"

Both had jeweled daggers at their belts. They drew
them and went light-footed to Gelmar. And Kell à Marg
said, "Tell your creatures to kill the man, Wandsman."

Desperately, furiously, Gelmar cried, "No, wait—"

For a moment, the beautiful men of the Citadel did
not know what to do. They all watched Gelmar and
waited.

Stark did not wait.

He spun around, swinging his clenched hands with
the iron weight of the manacles and the chain into the
body of the guard who was a little behind him to his
right. He felt the flesh break. The man's breath went out
in a harsh scream. He dropped and Stark hurdled him,
charging for the door. There were sudden shouts behind
him.

The two guards who were with Gerrith ran forward to
intercept him. Gerrith, forgotten for the moment, mov-

ing swiftly, snatched one of the small lamps from its pedestal and flung it at the wall.

Flaming oil splashed, spread, caught. The hangings, centuries dry, exploded into smoke and flame.

One of the guards turned back and struck Gerrith aside, much too late. Stark saw her fall and then he lost her. Smoke choked him, blinded him. Voices were rising in terror and urgent cries. The many faces of the Mother twisted, blackened, vanished. Two of the Diviners threw themselves upon the crystal, shielding it with their bodies. The others ran to beat futilely at the flames. One of the beautiful men was on fire; another, rushing to Gelmar's voice, blundered into Stark and went on without pausing. Stark called Gerrith's name but there was no answer, and then he stumbled over her. He caught her tunic and dragged her through the doorway, into the hall. A great gout of smoke came with them.

He thought for a moment she was dead. But she coughed and then said distinctly, "If you don't go now, this will be the end of it."

The tumult in the Hall grew louder as those inside fought their way toward the door. Students and acolytes came out of their chambers along the corridor. Stark bent over Gerrith.

She struck at him. "Get gone, damn you! I gave you this chance. Will you throw it away?"

Stark hesitated. Alone he might make it. Burdened with Gerrith, he could not. He touched her briefly. "If I live—" he said, and left her there, and ran.

He went down the corridor, huge and murderous, iron shackles swinging. White-furred bodies scattered before him or were swept aside. They were young, these student Diviners, and their teachers were old, and all were unused to combat. Stark went through them like a gale through chaff.

Behind him he heard fresh shouts and cries. Gelmar and Kell à Marg, at least, had won free of the burning Hall. Looking back, he saw two of the guards running after him. Them he could not fight, their swords against his irons.

He plunged into a branching corridor, running hard. A flight of rock-cut steps led him downward, into another corridor, dustier, more dimly lighted. He followed that into a maze of rooms, tunnels, and stairways, the rooms crowded with objects, the passages deserted, lighted by fewer and fewer lamps.

He stopped at last and listened. All he could hear now was the hammering of his own heart. For the moment, at least, he had lost them. He took one of the lamps from a wall niche and went on, deeper and deeper into the House of the Mother.

24

The Children must have spent innumerable generations gnawing away here in the bowels of the Witchfires. They must have been vastly more numerous than they were now, and Stark remembered Hargoth's comments on the necessity of fresh breeding stock. The Children would have cut themselves off from that, certainly by choice and probably by the alteration of their genes as well. Artificial mutants, they might be unable to cross-breed with humans. The Children of the Sea-Our-Mother might have undergone the same deprivation, but he had no way of judging that.

It was unpleasantly quiet. The silence of centuries hung here as thick as dust. Yet the air was breathable. The Children had seen to it that ventilation was adequate. Their engineering instincts had been sound as well, probably bred into them. They had a feeling for stone and how to use it. Their warren of caverns and passages seemed capable of enduring as long as the Witchfires.

Except for the lamp he carried, it was now totally dark. Stark moved on, having no idea where he was going, fighting down a growing panic. The House of the Mother would make a handsome tomb. Probably they would never even find his body.

In spite of that, curiosity as well as necessity compelled him to stop and examine some of the things that crammed these forgotten chambers.

He realized that he was in a museum.

What had Kell à Marg said? *We are students of the past. Historians.* They must have looted the dead and dying cities of the north. Perhaps even before they were abandoned by the people fleeing south in the Great Wandering, the Children had begun their collecting. Art objects, statuary, paintings, jewelry, musical instruments, fabrics, pots and pans, machines, toys, tools, books, constructions of wood and metal and plastic— anything of a size to be handled through the corridors, whole or piecemeal, and stored away in the caverns. The history and technology, art and ideas, of a totally destroyed civilization survived here in these buried vaults, the pleasure and the mania of a dying race.

Stark thought that whether he himself lived or died, the Children of Skaith-Our-Mother were going to have much trouble as time went by, trying to guard their incredible hoard.

He was looking for two things, a weapon and some tools to get the shackles off. There were plenty of weapons, most of them useless, lacking the technology that had made them work. Constant temperature and humidity had preserved most things remarkably well, but there was inevitable deterioration. He finally found a knife that did not come apart at the tang, and he thrust that into his belt.

The tools were easier. Mallet and chisel could endure a bit of punishment. But there was no way that he could use them by himself. He stuck the chisel in his belt beside the knife and carried the mallet. It made a serviceable weapon in itself.

There was no one to use it on.

Neither was there any water, nor any food. Thirst began to be a problem, with hunger not far behind. He was used to both, and he knew his potential. It would take him some time to die. But he ceased to reproach himself about Gerrith.

He had hoped to find another lamp, but they had all been neglected too long and the oil had evaporated. The level of the one he carried went slowly, steadily down.

He did not stop longer than he had to. He wanted to keep going as long as he had light.

Then, as he passed the mouth of a narrow tunnel, a strong draught of air blew it out.

The air was fresh and cold. Stark felt his way into the tunnel. After a little time he saw that there was light ahead. Daylight.

It came through an arched opening at the end of the tunnel. A wild surge of hope sent Stark running toward it.

Once lookouts might have been stationed here, keeping watch over the turbulent north. Or the Children might have taken the air after their work in the museum rooms, to see again the sun and the stars they had left behind. Now there was nothing but a high solitude. The tiny balcony was no more than a niche in the northern face of the Witchfires. Far too high, and that northern face too sheer, for any thought of getting down it.

Stark saw an immense white landscape, infinitely forbidding. From the feet of the Witchfires a naked plain tilted upward, gashed with the scars of old erosions. The wind blew fiercely across it, raising snow-devils that danced and whirled. Some of them had a peculiar look; these were not snow-devils at all, but pillars of steam rising out of the ground, to be shredded and torn away.

A thermal area. Stark became excited, remembering Hargoth's words about the magic mists that hid the Citadel. He looked up across the plain, to a distant range of mountains much higher and more cruel than the Witchfires. And he saw, to the northeast, low against the mountains' flank, a great boiling of white cloud.

He stood on his high lonely perch, and looked, and swore.

He saw, when he turned his head, a string of tiny figures moving across the vast whiteness of the plain, from the direction of the Witchfires.

Gelmar, going to the Citadel.

A driven man, Stark left the small niche. Turning his

back on the light, he went again into the darkness of the corridors.

Now he prayed for steps to lead him down. He had been trying from the first to work his way back to ground level, and he was appalled to find himself still so high. The devil of it was that, feeling his way along in the pitch blackness, he might be passing any number of steps to one side or the other without knowing it.

Hunger and thirst became more insistent. He was forced to stop now and again to sleep, as an animal sleeps, briefly but totally relaxed. Then he would get up and go on again, every nerve and every sense stretched fine to catch the slightest hint of anything that might guide him back to life.

He had slid and stumbled along what seemed like miles of passages, blundered horribly through crowded rooms that tried to swallow him in a tangle of relics, half fallen down infinite numbers of steps, when the faintest of faint sounds touched his ears.

He thought at first that it was only weariness, or the whisper of his own blood in his veins. Then it went away and he didn't hear it again. He had just come down a flight of steps. That was at his back. He could feel the carvings of a wall on both sides, so the corridor went ahead, and that must be where the sound had come from. He began padding along it, stopping frequently to hold his breath and listen.

The sound came again. It was unmistakable. It was music. Someone in this catacomb of dust and age and darkness was making music. Very peculiar music, atonal, twanging, quavering. It was the most beautiful music Stark had ever heard.

Twice more the music stopped, as though whoever was playing the instrument had halted in annoyance over a wrong note. Then it would begin again. Stark saw a gleam of light and approached without sound.

There was a carved doorway. Beyond was a small chamber well lighted by several lamps. One of the Children, an old man with slack skin and prominent bones, bent over an oddly shaped instrument with numerous strings. Beside him was an antique table strewn with ancient books and many parchments. There was also an untouched plate of food and a stone jug. The old man's fingers caressed the strings as if they were stroking a child.

Stark went in.

The old man looked up. Stark watched the slow advance of shock across his face.

"The Outside has come into the House of the Mother," he said. "It is the end of the world." And he set the instrument carefully aside.

"Not quite," said Stark. "All I want of the House of the Mother is to leave it. Is there a northern gate?"

He waited while the old man stared at him, great luminous eyes in a moth-eaten face, the fur of his crown rubbed up untidily, his whole being wrenched cruelly away from where it had been. Finally, Stark made a threatening movement.

"Is there a northern gate?"

"Yes. But I can't take you there."

"Why not?"

"Because I remember now. I was told—we were all told—an enemy, an outsider, was in the Mother's House and we were to watch. We were to give the alarm, if we should see him."

"Old man," said Stark, "you will not give the alarm, and you will take me to the northern gate." He placed his powerful hands on the frail instrument.

The old man stood up. In a soft and very desperate voice he said, "I am trying to recreate the music of Tlavia, Queen City of the High North before the Wandering. It is my life's work. That is the only Tlavian instrument known. The others are lost somewhere in the caverns. If it should be destroyed—"

"Consider yourself the guarantee of its safety," Stark

said. "If you do exactly as I tell you—" He took his hands away.

The old man was thinking. His thoughts were almost visible. "Very well," he said. "For the sake of the instrument."

Stark gave him the mallet and chisel. "Here." He laid his wrists on the antique table, which had a fine marble top and seemed sturdy. He regretted the sacrilege, but there was no other choice. "Get these things off me."

The old man was clumsy, and the table was considerably damaged, but in the end the manacles came off. Stark rubbed his wrists. Hunger and thirst had become painful. He drank from the stone bottle. It was some sort of dusty-tasting wine; he wished it had been water, but it was better than nothing. The food he thrust into his pockets, to be eaten along the way. The old man waited patiently. His acquiescence had been too quick, too unemotional. Stark wondered what mischief lurked in his transparent mind.

"Let us go," he said, and picked up the instrument.

The old man took a lamp and led the way into the corridor.

"Are there many like you?" Stark asked. "Solitary scholars?"

"Many. Skaith-Mother encourages scholars. She gives us peace and plenty so that we may spend our whole lives at our work. There are not so many of us as there used to be. Once there were a thousand at the study of music alone, thousands more at history, the ancient books, art and laws. And of course, the cataloguing." He sighed. "But it is a good life."

In a short time they were back in the inhabited areas. The old man did not have far to go to find his solitude. Stark took a firm hold on his worn harness with one hand, holding the instrument precariously in the other.

"If anyone sees us, old man," he said, "the music of Tlavia dies."

And the old man led him cunningly enough, skirting

the edges of the busy levels, the caverns of the lapidaries and goldsmiths, sculptors and stonemasons, the nurseries and schools for the young, the strange deep-buried farms where fungoid crops flourished in perpetual musty dampness. These lower levels, Stark noticed, were definitely warmer, and the old man explained that the thermal area extended beneath part of the Mother's House, giving them many gifts, such as hot water for the baths.

He also told Stark other things.

The nomad trail used by the Harsenyi ran between the pass of the Witchfires and the passes of the Bleak Mountains, the big range that Stark had seen. It was at the western side of the Plain of Worldheart; Stark remembered the little black dots of Gelmar's party moving along it. The trail was safe for the Harsenyi as long as they did not wander from it, and they had a permanent village in the foothills, which was as close as any of them ever got to the Citadel. The plain was called Worldheart because the Citadel was built on it, or above it. The old man had never seen the Citadel. He had never seen a Northhound. He thought that they did not range too far from the Citadel unless they were attracted by an intruder. They were said to be telepaths.

"They hunt in a pack," the old man said. "The kingdog's name is Flay. At least, it used to be. Perhaps the lead dog is always Flay. Or perhaps the Northhounds live forever."

Like the Lords Protector, Stark thought.

He felt a difference in the body of the old man, where his hand touched it. It had become tense, the breathing tight and rapid.

They were in a broad passageway, not very well lighted, obviously not much frequented. Ahead he could see the opening of another passage to the right.

The old man said innocently, "The northern gate is there, along that corridor. It's seldom used now. The Wandsmen used to come from the Citadel more often.

Now they come to the western gate, when they come at all." He held out his hands for the instrument.

Stark smiled. "Wait here, old man. No noise, not a word." Still carrying the frail instrument, Stark went noiselessly to the branching corridor and looked along it.

There was a great stone slab at the end of it, where it widened out into a guard chamber. And a guard was there. Half a dozen of the Children, male, young, armed, patently bored. Four of them were occupied with some game on a stone table. The other two watched.

The old man had begun to run. He did not even stop to see what became of his precious instrument. Stark set it down unharmed.

He took the knife from his belt and went down the corridor, moving fast, shoulders forward, all his attention fixed on that slab of rock that stood between him and freedom.

The Children probably had not had to fight in their own defense since the last of the Wandering. They were out of practice, babes comfortable and soft in the womb of the Mother. He was almost on top of them before they knew he was there. They sprang up to face him, eyes large with sudden fear, pawing for their weapons. They had not really believed that he would come. They had not really believed that if he did come he would try to kill them. Surely their six against his one—

They had not *really* understood what killing is.

Stark slashed one of the players across the throat. He fell across the table, tangling his mates with his thrashings, making dreadful noises. They stared at the blood, and Stark struck down another with his fist and caught up the light wiry body and threw it against the others. He went past them like a bull to the slab of stone and pushed against it. It moved. Two of them came at his back and he turned and fended them off, the knife blade and his heavy furs turning most of their sword cuts; their blades were light like their bodies, made more for beauty than for killing. He kept pressing his shoulder against the slab and it kept turning and in a moment they were hitting stone and he was through the opening. He slammed the stone shut on their screaming faces, and began to run.

They would spread the word through Kell à Marg's great House that he had escaped, but he did not think that anyone would come after him, at least not very far.

Not here on the Plain of Worldheart, where the Northhounds prowled.

25

Old Sun was below the peaks, and the northern face of the Witchfires was gray and ugly, a sheer frowning wall at his back. The mountain shadow made a long darkness across the plain. The wind was a knife, a scream, a madness bewailing eternal winter. The flogged snow-devils danced in desperation to appease it.

The region of boiling cloud that hid the Citadel was visible, small and bright against the flank of the Bleak Mountains, catching the last of the westering light.

The Citadel.

He did not know exactly how long he had been wandering in the House of the Mother, and the old man had not been able to tell him in terms that he could understand. They had their own view of time in those dark catacombs. But it was long enough for many things to have happened.

There was no point in asking himself questions for which there could be no answers until he reached the Citadel. If he reached it.

Stark fixed the bright patch of cloud as a mark in his mind's eye, northeast across the plain. He set out toward it.

The shadow of the Witchfires stretched longer and darker ahead of him. He would not outrun it. It would soon be night, and the Children were staying safe, as he had thought they would, in their Mother's House. Why risk their lives when the Northhounds would certainly deal with him? The Bleak Mountains burned with a bloody glow that dimmed quickly to ashen dullness. The first stars showed.

Stark lost his view of the Citadel-clouds and took his

bearing from a star. The whole landscape faded into that insubstantial bluish-gray that comes over the snow-lands at twilight, where everything slides away at the edges of sight. The sky turned darker, turned black. The Lamp of the North rose up in it, a huge green lantern, and the plain became white again, a diminished white but much more clearly seen now that the glimmery gray-ness had gone. The first twitching of the aurora appeared overhead.

Stark moved forward as steadily as he could, watching for the plumes of steam marking the thermal areas he had seen from the balcony. The wind tore at him, beat-ing him with hammer blows. It sent the snow-devils against him, and at these times he dropped face down on the ground until the blinding buffeting whirl of snow-dust passed over him. At other times the wind picked up low-er clouds of snow and mixed them cunningly with the thermal plumes so that all was a formless whiteness. Several times he stopped short, sensing a bareness and a tremor beneath his feet, to find a gaping blow-hole lying just ahead, ready to swallow him.

The ravines, those ancient gashes of erosion he had seen, were less dangerous. The bedrock of the plain was hard and had not scoured out too deeply. Wind and snow had worn the edges down. Nevertheless, Stark went carefully when he had to cross one. A fall here in the darkness of Worldheart could mean cheating the Northhounds of their pleasure.

He was happy, in a strange sort of way. The end of his journey was in sight, and he was free, unencumbered. His body and his skills were his to use to the limit, with-out regard for others. The battle against cold and wind and cruel terrain was a clean one, uncluttered by ideas, ideals, beliefs, or human spite. For the moment he was less Eric John Stark than he was N'Chaka, wild thing in a wild place, perfectly at home.

Perfectly at home, perfectly functional, wary and watchful. His gaze roved constantly, never straining against the night, never looking straight at an object but always past it, never trying to hold it steady, only sensing its shape and whether or not it moved.

Twice the wind brought him a hint of something other than the cold smells of snow and frozen ground.

The banners of the aurora snapped and quivered. The heads of the snow-devils seemed to touch them. Colors shifted, green, white, rose-fire. Plumes of steam shot high out of the rock, now to his right, now to his left, glimmering, shredding, vanishing. Sometimes he thought that dim white shapes stalked him between snow and steam. For a long while he could not be sure.

There came a time when there was no longer any doubt.

He had come, treading delicately, out of a cloud of mingled steam and snow, and he looked up along the tilt of the plain, and a great white thing stood there watching him.

Stark stopped. The thing continued to watch him. And a cold beast-thought touched his mind, saying,

I am Flay.

He was big. The ridge of his spine would have reached Stark's shoulder. His withers were high and powerful. The thick neck drooped with the weight of the massive head. Stark saw the eyes, large and unnaturally brilliant, the broad heavy muzzle, and the fangs, two white cruel rows of them, sharp as knives.

Flay stretched out a foreleg like a tree-trunk and unsheathed tiger claws. He tore five furrows in the frozen ground and smiled, lolling a red tongue.

I am Flay.

The eyes were bright. Bright. Hell-hound eyes

Swift panic overcame Stark, loosened his muscles, weakened his joints, dropped him helpless on the ground with cold nausea in his belly and a silent scream in his brain.

I am Flay.

And this is how they kill, Stark thought, with the fleeting remnants of sanity. Fear. A bolt of fear as deadly as any missile. This is how they were bred to kill. The size, the fangs and claws, are only camouflage. They do it with their minds.

He could not draw his knife.

Flay sauntered toward him. And now the other shapes were visible on the tilting plain, the pack, six, ten, a dozen, he couldn't count them, bounding and leaping, running.

Fear.

Fear was a sickness.

Fear was a dark wave rolling over him, taking sight and hearing, crushing mind and will.

He would never reach the Citadel, never see Gerrith. Flay would give him to the pack and they would play with him until he died.

I am Flay, said the cold beast-mind, and the red jaws laughed. Huge paws padded silently in the blowing snow.

Far down beneath the dark mass of fear that destroyed all human courage, another mind spoke. Cold beast-mind, not thinking or reasoning, mind alive and desperate to live, mind feeling self as bone and muscle, cold and pain, a hunger to be fed, a fear to be endured. Fear is life, fear is survival. The end of fear is death.

The cold beast-mind said, *I am N'Chaka.*

The blood beats, hot with living, hot with hate. Hate is a fire in the blood, a taste in the mouth of bitter salt.

I am N'Chaka.

I do not die.

I kill.

Flay paused, one tentative forefoot lifted. He swung his head from side to side, puzzled.

The human thing ought now to be inert and helpless. Instead it spoke to him; it groped and tottered and rose from the ground, rose to its hands and knees and faced him.

I am N'Chaka.

The pack halted their playful rush. They formed a semicircle behind Flay, growling.

Fear, said Flay's mind. *Fear.*

They sent fear, deadly killing fear.

Cold beast-mind let the fear slide over it. Cold beast-eyes saw Flay, coarse-furred Flay looming in the night-gleaming.

I have seen the great rock lizard open his jaws to take me, and he has not taken me. Why should I fear you?

The pack growled, looking sidelong. *Flay, Flay! This is not a human!*

The N'Chaka thing got to its hind legs, crouching. It circled, making beast sounds. It sprang at Flay.

Flay struck it sprawling with one sweep of his paw.

The thing rolled over twice. Blood came out of rents in its fur. It bounded up and drew the knife from its belt. It came again at Flay.

The pack could not understand. Human victims did not fight. They did not challenge the king-dog, only a member of the pack did that. This thing was not a member of the pack, but neither was it human. They did not know what it was.

They sat down to watch, while N'Chaka fought the king-dog for his life.

They would not send more fear. This was up to Flay.

Flay had realized, not believing it, that fear was useless. He tried once more, but the N'Chaka thing came at him without pause, slashing at him, dodging, circling, darting in and out, wary now of the claws. It was fighting; there was nothing left in its mind but fight, fight and kill.

It enjoyed the fighting. It meant to kill.

Now it was Flay who feared.

In all his long life he had never failed to take his prey cleanly. No single victim had ever fought back.

Now this N'Chaka thing defied him. And the pack was watching, and he had no weapons but his claws and teeth.

And those he was not used to using, except in play. None of the young dogs had yet dared to challenge him.

Fear! he said to the pack. *Send fear!*

They only watched, moving restlessly, the wind tearing at their fur.

In a fury, Flay struck at the N'Chaka thing with his terrible claws.

The thing was ready this time. It leapt back and slashed with the knife. It slashed so that Flay howled and went on three legs.

The pack smelled his blood and whined.

A measure of humanity was creeping back into Stark's mind, now that he had mastered the fear. And along with it came a savage sense of triumph.

The Northhounds were not invincible.

Perhaps the Citadel would not be invincible, either.

Because he knew now that he was going to reach it.

He knew that he was going to kill Flay.

Flay knew it too.

The wounded paw had slowed the Northhound. But he was still formidable. He bared the double row of fangs and made rushes. His jaws snapped on empty air with a frightening sound. They would crush a man's thigh-bone like a dry stick. Stark circled him, making him turn against that bad foot, and twice he darted in and slashed at the face. His eyes held Flay's eyes, the hell-hound eyes that were bred for terror, and he thought. *How close the knife comes, Flay! How it flashes! Soon—*

The heavy head dropped lower. The terrible eyes wanted to look away. The paw bled and the pack whined, red tongues hanging.

Stark feinted, ceased to hold Flay's eyes, and the big head turned aside. Stark flung himself onto Flay's high bony back.

He was only there for a second or two before he was thrown off, but that was long enough for the knife to go in. Flay whirled, snapping at the hilt standing out behind his shoulder, and then he staggered and went down and blood came out of his mouth.

Stark pulled out the knife and let the pack have the

body. He stood apart, waiting. Their shallow minds had already told him what they would do.

He waited until they were finished.

They gathered then, keeping their eyes carefully averted lest they should seem to challenge him. The largest of the young dogs came belly down and licked Stark's hand.

You will follow me?

You killed Flay. We follow.

But I am human.

Not human. You are N'Chaka.

You guard the Citadel.

Against humans.

And how many lost and hungry wayfarers have those jaws snapped up, Stark wondered. The Lords Protector defended their privacy too well. *You defend against humans, but not against N'Chaka?*

We could not kill N'Chaka.

Will you kill Wandsmen?

No.

They had neither love nor loyalty, but their breeding held them true. Fair enough.

The other men, who serve the Wandsmen?

They are nothing to us.

Good.

He considered their well fleshed bodies. There were certainly not enough human victims to keep them fat, and there was little game on the Plain of Worldheart where they ranged. Someone must feed them.

Where do you kennel?

At the Citadel.

Come, then.

With the pack at his heels, Stark set off toward the mountains.

26

The boiling clouds turned copper with the rising of Old Sun. The Northhounds trotted unconcerned through a wilderness of humped rock and gaping blow-holes. Stark went with them while the ground boomed and shook and the steam spurted.

He had not planned it this way. He had not thought that a direct attack on the Citadel would be possible. But this unexpected, and highly uncertain, weapon had been put into his hand, and he had decided to use it.

Now.

As swiftly and brutally as possible.

The thermal area seemed to go on forever. Then suddenly they had passed through it, and the mountains were there, and the Citadel.

Dark and strong and solid, clinging to the mountain flank, the compact shape of its walls and towers looking like an outcrop of the native rock. The fortress and fountainhead, from which a handful of men ruled a planet.

He could understand why it had been built here, hidden behind its perpetual curtain. In the days of the Wandering, when everything was chaos, this place would have been isolated from the main streams of migration, and therefore relatively safe. Tall crags protected the Citadel at back and side, the thermal pits guarded its front. With all that, and the Northhounds, the Lords Protector need not have worried overmuch about bands of plunderers coming south over the passes. From the size of the Citadel, they would have garrisoned fewer than a hundred men, and they would not have needed more.

How many men would be there now, after all these centuries of peace? He did not know. He looked at the Northhounds and hoped that they would be adequate. Otherwise, any number would be too many against one man with a knife.

There were sentries on the walls, bright-eyed men with blank faces. They saw Stark at the edge of the cloud with the pack behind him, and even over the roaring of the vent-holes Stark could hear their sudden shouting.

Hurry! he told the Northhounds.

No hurry, said the young dog, whose name was Gerd.

The Northhounds trotted on toward the base of the Citadel, courses of stone laid in upon the rock.

They will kill you, Stark told them, and ran, dodging this way and that.

Arrows began to fly from the walls. In the roiling copper shadow they flew. None hit Stark, though he felt the wind of them. Some stuck in the ground. Two hit Northhounds.

I said they would kill you.

He was under the base of the Citadel now, where the arrows could not reach him.

Why, N'Chaka?

It was a cry of puzzled anguish. The Northhounds began to run.

They believe you have come to attack them.

We have always been faithful.

A third hound rolled over screaming, an arrow through his flanks.

They doubt you now.

And small wonder. For the first time since the first whelp of them was born, they had let in an intruder. They had *brought* in an intruder.

The Northhounds bayed.

There was a hole in the rock. They ran into it. The

cave was large and dry, sheltered from the wind. It
smelled of kennel and there were troughs where the
hounds were fed. At the back was a door of thick iron
bars with heavy bolts on the inner side.

Stark went to the door. He could sense the bewilder-
ment and rage in their beast minds.

*They tried to kill you. Why did you not send fear to
them?*

Gerd growled and whimpered. He was one of the first
two hit. The arrow had gashed his rump painfully. *We
never sent fear to those. We will now.*

Stark reached through to the bolts and began to draw
them.

Are there humans in the Citadel?

Gerd answered irritably, *With Wandsmen.*

If they were with the Wandsmen, or the Lords Protector, it was no concern of Gerd's.

*But there are humans? You can touch their minds?
Human. One mind. Touch.*

One mind. One human.

Gerrith?

Halk?

Ashton?

Stark opened the door. *Come and kill for N'Chaka.*
They came.

There was a hall with storerooms on either side, and
then a rough stair that went up into darkness. Stark
climbed as fast as he dared, much faster than was wise,
his knife in his hand. The people of the Citadel were
surprised, shocked, off-guard, and he wanted to use that
advantage. At the top was a massive iron door to be
shut if anyone managed to pass living through the
Northhound's kennel, and a windlass arrangement to
drop a section of the stair. Beyond was a chamber clut-
tered with the debris of long occupancy, things working
their way down the scale to eventual burial in the thermal pits. A barred slit let in daylight, which was only a little better than no light at all.

A broader stair led up from this room, into a long low hall lighted at intervals by lamps. There were no windows. Row upon row of wooden racks crammed the space, leaning and sagging under the weight of endless rolls of parchment.

The records, Stark guessed, of generations of Wandsmen who had come to the Citadel to report and confer concerning their work in the world.

They looked as though they would burn well. So did the enormous timbers that sustained the roof.

There was a stair on the opposite side of the hall. He was halfway to it when a body of men came plunging down. They might have been on their way to close that iron door.

They stopped dead when they saw the Northhounds. The hounds never came inside the Citadel. They could not conceive of such a thing happening. Yet it had happened.

Their faces and their bright eyes remained expressionless even after the Northhounds had sent fear.

Kill, said Stark, and the pack killed. They were very angry, very swift. When they had finished, he picked up a sword, leaving belt and scabbard untouched. The sword would wipe clean.

He started up the stair.

Gerd spoke in his mind. *N'Chaka. Wandsmen—*

He saw *white* in his mind and knew that Gerd meant the Lords Protector. The hounds did not distinguish between Wandsmen.

Wandsmen say kill you.

He had expected this. The hounds were loyal to the Wandsmen. How strong was his own hold over them? If the Wandsmen were stronger, he would finish here as the blank-faced men had finished.

He turned to Gerd, looking straight into the hell-hound eyes.

You cannot kill N'Chaka.

Gerd stared at him steadily. The bristled lips pulled

back to show the rows of fangs. There was still blood on them. The pack whined and whimpered, clawing the stones.

Who do you follow? Stark asked.

We follow the strongest. But Flay obeyed Wandsmen—

I am not Flay. I am N'Chaka. Shall I kill you as I killed Flay?

He would have done it. The sword point was aimed straight for Gerd's throat and he was as hungry for blood as they were.

Gerd knew it. The fiery gaze slid aside. The head hung down. The pack became quiet.

Send fear, Stark said. *Drive away all but the Wandsmen and the human. Drive away the servants who kill you. Then we will talk to the Wandsmen.*

Not kill?

Not the Wandsmen, not the human. Talk.

But Stark's hand gripped the sword.

The Northhounds obeyed him. He felt the air vibrate with their sending.

He led them up the stair.

Some men were at the top. Terror was on them, an agony in the gut. The Northhounds tore them leisurely. Gerd picked up the leader and carried him in his jaws like a kitten.

No one else stood against them. All the others had had strength enough to run.

Stark came at length into another hall, higher than the one that held the records but not so long, with windows open onto the eternal mist. It was sparsely furnished, ascetic, a place for meditation. Kell à Marg, spiteful daughter of Skaith, had been wrong. There was no hint here of secret sin and luxury, either in the hall or in the faces of the seven white-robed men who stood there in attitudes of arrested motion, overwhelmed by the swiftness with which this thing had happened.

There was an eighth man, not wearing a white robe.

Simon Ashton.

Gerd dropped what he was carrying. Stark put his left hand on the hound's great head and said, "Let the Earthman come to me."

Ashton came and stood at Stark's right hand. He was thinner than Stark remembered and he showed the strain of long captivity. Otherwise he seemed unhurt.

Stark said to the Lords Protector, "Where is Gerrith?"

The foremost of them answered. Like the others, he was an old man. Not aged or infirm, but old in work and dedication as well as years. His thin hard jaw and fierce eyes reflected an uncompromising and inflexible toughness.

"We questioned her, and the wounded man, and then sent them south with Gelmar. It was not believed that you could survive the Children in the House of the Mother."

He looked at the Northhounds. "This too would not have been believed."

"Nevertheless," said Stark, "I am here."

And now that he was here, he wondered what he was going to do with them. They were old men. Unyielding old men, devoted to their principles, ruling with the iron rod of righteousness, cruel only to be kind. He hated them. If they had killed Ashton he could have killed them, but Ashton was alive and safe and he could not see himself slaughtering them in cold blood.

There was another factor. The Northhounds. They felt his thoughts and growled, and Gerd leaned his massive shoulder against Stark's side, to hold him.

The man in white smiled briefly. "That instinct, at least, is too strong for you. They will not let you kill us."

"Go, then," said Stark. "Take your servants and go. Let the people of Skaith see the Lords Protector for what they are, not gods or immortals but only seven old men cast adrift in the world. I will pull down this Citadel."

"You may destroy it. You cannot destroy what it stands for. It will remain a symbol. You cannot destroy us, for the work we do is greater than our physical bodies. The prophecy is false, man from the stars. You will not prevail. We shall continue to serve our people."

He paused. "My name is Ferdias. Remember it."

Stark nodded. "I'll remember. And prophecy or not, Ferdias, you have served too long."

"And what do you serve? The littleness of one man. For one man, you set our world in turmoil." He looked at Ashton.

"He too is only a symbol," said Stark softly. "The symbol of reality. That is what you're fighting, not one man, or two. Go and fight it, Ferdias. Wait for the stars to crash in on you. Because they will."

They turned and left him. He stared after their proud and stubborn backs, and the Northhounds held him, whimpering.

"You are a fool, Eric," Ashton said, and shook his head. "As Ferdias said, it does seem a lot for one man."

"Well," said Stark, "before we're done, you may wish I'd left you with the Lords Protector. What made them decide against killing you?"

"I convinced them I'd be more valuable to them alive. They're very worried men, Eric. They know they're threatened by something big, but they don't know how big. They don't really understand. The whole concept of space-flight and the Galactic Union is too new and strange. Really shattering. They don't know how to deal with it, and they thought I might be of some help to them since I'm part of it. I pointed out that they could always kill me later on."

He looked at the Northhounds and shivered. "I won't ask you how you did that. I'm afraid I know."

"Of all men, you ought to," said Stark, and smiled. Then he asked, "How long ago did Gelmar leave, with Gerrith?"

"It was yesterday."

"They won't have got far ahead of us, then. Not with Halk slowing them down. Simon, I know that the Ministry cannot condone the vandalism I am about to commit, but you won't try to stop me, will you?"

Again Ashton looked at the pack. "Not likely. Your friends might be annoyed."

Stark set about destroying the Citadel as well as he could, and it was well enough. The furnishings, the hall of records, and the great timber beams burned hotly. Most of the outer walls would be left, but the interior would not be habitable, and in any case the sacred isolation of the Citadel was gone for all time, as was the superstitious awe that went with it.

He thought the destruction of the Lords Protector might be just as complete. He was glad, when he considered it, that he had not been able to kill them. They would have remained forever a potent and holy legend. The truth, when the people saw it, would kill them more certainly than the sword.

The Northhounds did not attempt to interfere with his burning of the Citadel. Their guardianship seemed to have been associated only with the pleasurable aspects of keeping intruders away from it.

Stark stood with Ashton on the road outside the Citadel, watching the flames lick at the window-places, and he said,

"So far, so good. There is still Gerrith, and a long walk south, and then we'll see what we can do about Irnan and the freedom of the stars. Not to speak of getting ourselves safely away from Skaith."

"It's a large order," said Ashton.

"We have allies." Stark turned to the Northhounds, to Gerd. *What will you do now that there is nothing left for you to guard?*

We will follow the strongest, said Gerd, licking Stark's hand.

And so you will, thought Stark, until I fall sick or

wounded, and then you will do to me as you did to Flay. Or try to.

He bore them no ill-will for that. It was their nature. He laid his hand on Gerd's head.

Come, then.

With Ashton at his side, Stark set his face to the passes of the Bleak Mountains and the Wandsmen's Road beyond. Somewhere on that road was Gerrith, and at its end, the starships waited.